THE *Silver Kiss*

THE
Silver Kiss

ANNETTE CURTIS KLAUSE

DELACORTE PRESS

Published by Delacorte Press
an imprint of Random House Children's Books
a division of Random House, Inc.
New York

This is a work of fiction. Names, characters, places, and incidents either
are the product of the author's imagination or are used fictitiously. Any
resemblance to actual persons, living or dead, events, or locales is
entirely coincidental.

Delacorte Press and colophon are registered trademarks of
Random House, Inc.

www.randomhouse.com/teens

Educators and librarians, for a variety of teaching tools,
visit us at www.randomhouse.com/teachers

The Library of Congress has cataloged the hardcover edition of this work
as follows:

Klause, Annette Curtis.
The silver kiss / by Annette Curtis Klause.
p. cm.
Summary: A mysterious teenage boy harboring a dark secret helps Zoë
come to terms with her mother's terminal illness.
ISBN 978-0-385-30160-2
[1. Vampires—Fiction. 2. Death—Fiction.] I. Title
PZ7.K67815Si 1990
[Fic]—dc20   89-48880
CIP   AC

ISBN 978-0-385-73422-6 (trade pbk)
ISBN 978-0-385-90435-3 (GLB)

Printed in the United States of America

10 9 8 7 6 5 4 3 2 1

First Trade Paperback Edition

To Larry Callen, who talked me into writing a novel; and to the Tuesday Night Writing Group, who kept me going—you know who you are.

· 1 ·

Zoë

The house was empty. Zoë knew as soon as she walked through the front door. Only a clock ticking in the kitchen challenged the silence.

Fear uncurled within her. Mommy, she thought like a child. Is it the hospital again—or worse? She dropped her schoolbag in the hall, forgetting the open door, and walked slowly into the kitchen, afraid of what message might await her. There was a note on the refrigerator:

> Gone to the hospital. Don't worry. Make
> your dinner. Be back when I can.
> Love, Dad.
> P.S. Don't wait up.

She crumpled the note and flung it at the trash can. It missed. She snorted in disgust. It seemed that lately all her conversations with her father had been carried on with a

Zoë

banana refrigerator magnet as intermediary. The banana speaks, she thought. It defended the refrigerator, stopped her from opening the door. She couldn't eat.

Zoë the Bird they called her at school. She had always been thin, but now her bones seemed hollow. Her wrists and joints were bruised with shadows. She was almost as thin as her mother, wasting away with cancer in the hospital. A sympathy death perhaps, she wondered half seriously. She had always been compared to her mother. She had the same gray eyes, long black hair with a slight curl, and deceptively pale skin that tanned quickly at the slightest encouragement. Wouldn't it be ironic if she died, too, fading out suddenly when her look-alike went?

Zoë drifted from the kitchen, not sure what to do. How could she wash dishes or wipe counters when God knows what was happening with her mother at the hospital? She shrugged off her coat, leaving it on a chair. Dad kept on saying everything would be all right, but what if something happened and she wasn't even there, all because he couldn't admit to her that Mom might be dying?

She tugged at her sweater, twisted a lock of hair; her hands couldn't keep still. I should be used to this by now, she thought. It had been going on for over a year: the long stays in the hospital, short stays home, weeks of hope, then sudden relapses, and the cures that made her mother sicker than the pain. But it would be a sin to be used to something like that, she thought. Unnatural. You can't let yourself get used to it, because that's like giving in.

She paused in the dining room. It was sparsely furnished with a long antique trestle table and chairs that almost all matched, but the walls were a fanfare to her mother's life. They gave a home to the large, bright, splashy oils that Anne Sutcliff painted; pictures charged with bold emotions, full of laughing people who leapt and swirled and sang. Like Mom, Zoë thought—like Mom used to. And that's where they differed, for Zoë wrote quiet poetry suffused with twilight and questions. It's not even good poetry, she thought. I don't have talent, it's her. I should be the one ill; she has so much to offer, so much life. "You're a dark one," her mother said sometimes with amused wonder. "You're a mystery."

I want to be like them, she thought almost pleadingly as she stroked the crimson paint to feel the brush strokes, hoping maybe to absorb its warmth.

The living room was cool and shadowed. The glints of sunlight on the roof she could see through the window resembled light playing on the surface of water, and the room's aqua colors hinted at undersea worlds. Perhaps she'd find peace here. She sank into the couch.

Just enjoy the room, she told herself; the room that has always been here, and always will; the room that hasn't changed. I am five, she pretended. Mom is in the kitchen making an early dinner. They are going out tonight to a

3

party, and Sarah is coming over to baby-sit. I'll go and play with my dollhouse soon.

But it wouldn't last, so she opened her eyes and stretched. Her fingers touched the sleek cheapness of newsprint. The morning paper was still spread on the couch. She glanced at it with little interest, but the headline glared: MOTHER OF TWO FOUND DEAD. Her stomach lurched. Everyone's mother found dead, she thought bitterly. Why not everyone's? But she couldn't help reading the next few lines. Throat slashed, the article said, drained dry of blood.

"That's absurd," she said aloud. Her fingers tightened in disgust, crumpling the page. "What is this—the *National Enquirer*?" She tossed the paper away, wrenched herself to her feet, and headed for her room.

But the phone rang before she reached the stairs. She flinched but darted for the hall extension and picked it up. It was a familiar voice, but not her father's.

"Zoë, it's horrible." Lorraine, her best friend, wailed across the phone lines with typical drama. It should have been comforting.

"What's horrible?" Zoë gasped with pounding heart. Had the hospital phoned Lorraine's house because she wasn't home?

"We're moving."

"What?" A moment's confusion.

"Dad got that job in Oregon."

"Oregon? My God, Lorraine. Venus."

Zoë

"Almost."

Zoë sat down in the straight-backed chair beside the phone table. It wasn't her father. It wasn't death calling, but . . . "When?" she asked.

"Two weeks."

"So soon?" Zoë wrapped and unwrapped the phone cord around her fist. This isn't happening, she thought.

"They want him right away. He's flying out tonight. Can you believe it? He's going to look for a house when he gets there. I got home and Diane was calling up moving companies."

"But you said he wasn't serious."

"Shows how much he tells me, doesn't it? Diane knew."

Zoë grasped for something to say. Couldn't something stop this? "Isn't she freaked at the rush?"

"Oh, *she* thinks it's great. It's a place nuclear fallout will miss, and she can grow lots of zucchini."

"What about your mom?"

"She wouldn't care if he moved to Australia. But she's pretty pissed that he's taking me."

"Can't you stay with her?" Please, please, Zoë begged silently.

"Oh, you know. That's a lost battle. Cramp her style."

"Lorraine! She's not that bad."

"She moved out, didn't she?"

Zoë

No use fighting that argument again, Zoë thought. "Oregon." She sighed.

Lorraine groaned. "Yeah! This is hideous. It's the wilderness or something. I'm not ready for the great trek. I could stay with you," she added hopefully.

"I'll ask," Zoë said, although there wasn't a chance. They both knew that was impossible right now.

"Nah!"

What will I do? Zoë thought. "You can visit." It seemed a pathetic suggestion.

"Big deal!"

"Yeah."

"Can you come over?" Lorraine asked.

"No. I better stay here for now."

"Uh-oh! Something wrong?"

"She's in the hospital again."

"Oh, hell."

This is where Lorraine shuts down, Zoë thought. Why can't she talk to me about it? Why does she have to back off every time? She's my best friend, damn it, not like those nerds at school who are too embarrassed even to look at me anymore. She searched for what she wanted to say. Something to keep Lorraine on the line.

There was silence.

"Listen," said Lorraine, "you don't really feel like talking now. Call me later when you've heard. Okay?"

No, it's you who doesn't want to talk, Zoë thought, but she found herself saying, "Uh-huh."

Zoë

"Okay. We'll talk then." But she didn't hang up. "Hey, listen, Zoë, I love you and all that mush. Like sisters, you know." It tumbled out fast to cover the unaccustomed shyness. "Call me."

"Sure." Zoë smiled wryly. They wouldn't talk about it. "Bye."

"Bye, Zo. Hold tight," Lorraine whispered before she hung up.

She does care, Zoë reassured herself. She just doesn't know how to deal with it. Who does? But Zoë was angry anyway. They could always talk before. Usually Lorraine's choice of topic, but they could talk. And now, Lorraine leaving. Was the world coming to an end? They'd been friends forever. What's wrong with the way things were? Why did you have to go and change every damn thing? she felt like yelling at a God she wasn't even sure existed. Am I being punished? What did I do?

It all made her so very tired. I'm ready to take a nap, she decided. She went upstairs. Sleeping had taken the place of eating lately. She lay down on top of the spread and escaped for a while.

She awoke with a jolt. She grappled with the fleeting blur of dreams and recognized sounds that might have been the front door slamming, or the thud of her own room's door. She got up stiff and unrested and made her way downstairs. Rattling and crackling came from the kitchen. She entered to find her father making himself a

7

bowl of cereal. White-faced, he looked at her, dark circles etched beneath his eyes.

"Dammit, Zoë, the front door was open."

"Sorry, Dad. I must have forgotten. No one was here. It scared me. I went to find a note." Her fingers picked nervously at the seam of her jeans. How could she have forgotten the door?

"You can't just leave doors open, Zoë. For crying out loud, look at the newspapers."

Newspapers? she thought. Was he talking about that article? Why bring that up? Why was he picking on her? He didn't care. "I was here."

"I know. I saw your bag. I checked your room." His voice softened. "Sleeping again, Zo? Don't you sleep at night?"

She didn't answer. If he was home any amount of time, he would know.

The sight of his cereal made her hungry at last. She looked in the refrigerator. A tuna casserole her mother's friend Carol had brought over three days ago sat there, browning around the edges. Carol was a warm, generous person, but she was not a cook. Zoë shut the casserole safely away and sat down with her father. She served herself some cereal too. She thought she could handle cereal.

Her father was staring at her. She suddenly felt sorry for being a bitch. He looked sad. It wasn't his fault he had to

Zoë

spend so much time at the hospital, so much time making up work, so he could pay for a private room. Maybe if all his side of the family weren't off in California it would be easier on him. He should let me help more, she thought. But she could hear exactly what he would say. You can help by not worrying your mother.

"How's Mom?" She hardly dared ask.

"Not too good this time, love. She's still trying to be a good soldier, but it's wearing thin."

"Is she staying?" Please say no, Zoë thought.

"Yes, a few weeks. Maybe more."

Zoë saw the pinched look on his face, and the tears behind his eyes. Maybe forever, she thought. Yes, it's forever this time, but he can't tell me.

They both ate silently and mechanically. There was no enjoyment, just the surrender to physical need. Her dad had turned back into Harry Sutcliff, the man whose wife was dying, the man who had forgotten he had a daughter.

Several times she took a breath to speak, but the words died in her throat. "Dad?" she finally said hesitantly.

"Hmm?" His gaze was distant.

"Dad. About Lorraine."

"What? Had a fight?" he answered vaguely.

This isn't grade school, she wanted to yell, but she said quietly, carefully, "She's moving." Suddenly she was almost crying. All it would take would be his arms around her, and she wanted that badly.

"Hey, that's exciting," he said, missing the point. He slurped his milk absently.

The tears stayed backed up tight. A lump hurt her throat, and she wanted to scream it out. Where was the old Dad who might have said, "Well, tell her to stand still." He would have laughed at his own joke, then turned serious to hear her out and comfort her. He didn't always understand like her mother did, but he tried. I guess he's in there somewhere, she thought. She didn't try to tell him again. His world was too shattered for her to add her own cracked pieces to the pile.

Mom would know what to say, Zoë thought. Even now, she would. If only they wouldn't cut my visits so short. It seemed like she'd no sooner remembered what she wanted to say than they were hustling her out the door again. No one listened to her.

"I'm going out for a walk," she said abruptly. She had to walk or she'd scream for sure. She got her denim jacket from the hall closet. "Bye!"

"Don't be too long," her father called.

Doesn't he realize what time it is? she asked herself as she walked up the street. Almost ten. What happened to worrying about "the newspapers"?

The night was crisp and sweet like apples. A gibbous moon hung plump and bright. She headed for the small

10

Zoë

local park. It was a plot of land on a street corner, scattered with trees and holding a thick maze of bushes near the center. There were a few swings, a slide, a seesaw, and three battered animals on springs that bobbed you back and forth drunkenly, until your backside grew too sore to sit on them.

Zoë loved to come late and wander alone after even the wild children had been dragged home. She dreaded the advent of the bright lights the safety-conscious community wanted to install. She liked it as it was now, with the few lights making golden pools in the mysterious darkness.

She settled on her favorite of the three heavily etched benches. It faced the gazebo not far away, at the very center of the park. The pretty little domed building had always fascinated her. It had sets of steps all around like a carousel, and its open gingerbread sides were barely walls. It was always kept freshly painted summer-white and reminded her of a tiny palace from an Indian fairy tale. She had heard that bands used to play there once, on Sunday afternoons; now children sheltered there when it rained. Take me into your story, she thought.

Moonlight lit the gazebo, tracing it with silver, but a shadow crept inside, independent of natural shades. She tensed. Her hands gripped the edge of the bench. She leaned forward to decipher its meaning, peering into the mottled dark. She saw someone within.

Zoë

A figure detached from the shadows. Her mouth dried. Mother of two found dead, she thought. It moved toward her, stepped into the moonlight on the side closest to her, and briefly she thought to run. Then she saw his face.

He was young, more boy than man, slight and pale, made elfin by the moon. He noticed her and froze like a deer before the gun. They were trapped in each other's gaze. His eyes were dark, full of wilderness and stars. But his face was ashen. Almost as pale as his silver hair.

With a sudden ache she realized he was beautiful. The tears that prickled her eyes broke his bonds, and he fled, while she sat and cried for all things lost.

· 2 ·

Simon

Simon wiped the rat's blood from around his mouth. It was not as satisfying as human blood, but it would do. There had been no food at the park, except the girl, of course. She had surprised him. He didn't like surprises. But now he remembered the way she had held him with her eyes, and the slight taste of fear on the night air. He regretted having left so fast.

He had crouched in this alley behind a row of shops for twenty minutes now, catching and drinking, catching and drinking. They were hiding now, the rats. They knew something was up. Big cat, he thought, and smiled a thin, glittering smile.

Time to move on. He stood and stretched, lean-muscled arms reaching skyward. He wore only a T-shirt despite the cool fall night. It was black like his jeans, like the high-top Chucks trimmed with white. He was fond of black. Shad-

13

Simon

ows, he thought. Night. It satisfied him to wear black, yet
his laces were red. "Blood," he had whispered that evening at the thrift store, when his fingers would not leave
them alone in the bin. They tangled around his nervous
hand until he had to fling them from him or buy them. He
handed a dime from the gutter over to the woman with the
suspicious frown and fled to this same alley to put them
on.

Where would he go from here? The park? Maybe that
girl had left by now. But maybe not. I should go anyway,
he thought, and smiled again, the same glittering smile.
She was beautiful, dark like the night, but thin, as if one
of his brethren had already claimed her. A frown changed
his features suddenly, then disappeared as quickly. No.
She did not have the smell of that upon her. There was
something voluptuous about her, though, that reminded
him of death. Big breasts, too, he thought, and chuckled at
his peculiarly human preference.

But she had startled him. He had found that park
two weeks ago, and no one came at that time of night.
He had let his guard slip. That was dangerous, foolish.
No, he would not go to the park, he decided. It would
keep. She had sat there with a familiarity that suggested
habit. He would see her again. He would go to that house
instead. He had only a few blocks to walk from here. He
would see what that boy was up to.

Simon left the alley cautiously. It was not good to be
seen at the same place often. It was an excellent hunting

place; he did not want to lose it. He walked the pavement with shoulders hunched, hands in jeans pockets, as if against the cold. Who knew who was watching? He would have to get a coat. The street he traveled intersected the alley that ran behind the houses on Chestnut Street. He made a right. Five houses along he stopped at the end of a long backyard.

There were no lights on at the back of the house. The yard was mottled with moonlight. Simon flowed from shadow to shadow, between trees and bushes, as if a shadow himself. He might have been a cloud in front of the moon. He reached the rough brick of the house and crept to the oak tree at the corner. With the ease of a cat he scaled the tree and flowed up to a perch on a sturdy limb. He barely rattled the brittle autumn leaves that still clung tenaciously to their twigs.

He could see into a bedroom. It was an anonymous room. The walls were bare, nothing there to suggest the personality of the occupant. But there was an occupant, a small huddle on the bed. A boy of about six or seven curled with a book, reading by moonlight with a teddy bear close beside him. You'll ruin your eyesight, boy, Simon thought, and grinned wickedly. It was a thicker book than you would expect a six-year-old to be reading, and Simon itched to see the title. Occasionally, the boy would suppress a laugh and shake his head, whisking his delicate white hair through the moonlight.

Then the door opened. Gold stole silver as the hall light

shone into the room. A young woman stood in the door-way, smiling as she caught the last flurry of the book being concealed under the covers.

"Christopher," she said softly, "it's a little late to be playing. It's nearly midnight. Settle down, dear. Get some sleep."

"Uh-huh," the boy answered, and snuggled into his pillow. She blew him a kiss and left, closing the door.

Simon saw the boy lying there with his eyes open, staring into the night, still defying sleep, still smiling. There was a growl in the back of Simon's throat he could barely contain. It almost choked him. He climbed down the tree before it burst from his mouth. It was not the right time or place.

Below, there was a clatter in the kitchen. Dishes were being put into the dishwasher, and two sleepy voices were talking. He listened close to the window.

". . . should have settled in by now," came a man's voice.

"But it's hard for a young child," the woman answered, "adjusting to a new home."

"It's been a month."

"Yes, but after a year in that home, and God knows what before?"

"Yeah, guess you're right."

"He's a sweet boy."

"A bit quiet."

"Oh, he'll be a brain. You'll see."

The man laughed. "Got it all planned out, have you?"

"Sure. Nobel prize."

He laughed again. "Come on. Let's go to bed." The light went out.

"It'll work out, you'll see," said the woman. "You can't expect perfect when you adopt an older child."

"Yeah. It's a pity about that delicate skin as well. Too damn sensitive. Maybe if we . . ." His voice faded into the center of the house.

Simon sat in the bushes for a long while. He breathed the night, made plans, and abandoned them. No one in the house stirred. Dreams shimmered in the windows; all except one window, where dark hunger beckoned.

Finally, Simon heard the first predawn bird cry, and he rose to his feet in a single supple motion. His body made no protest at the breaking of the vigil. It was as if it were only seconds ago he had crouched there to watch. Silently, he left the yard by the way he had come and, accompanied by awakening birds, made his way back to what was home this week—an abandoned elementary school on Jennifer Street.

He pulled aside a board and slid through a smashed window into the principal's office. The room, begrimed with dust and cobwebs, had once been a synonym for hell to sixth graders, but now all that was left was an old file cabinet with only one drawer working and a desk with rusted seams. There was no chair. Built-in shelves lined the room, and the wooden floor had once been handsome. A battered suitcase sat on one of the shelves.

With the board back in place the room was dark. The dawn found its way through the planks here and there, needle-thin rays spotlighting dancing dust motes, but they barely penetrated the dark. This did not bother Simon. He did not need much light to see. He took down the suitcase, put it on the desk, and opened it. Inside was a small painting in a gilt frame. It was a family group: a man, a woman with a baby in her arms, and a small child. The varnish was cracked and old. Beneath the painting was soil, dark dry soil almost as flyaway as the dust of the room. Simon ran his fingers through it and sighed. This was his sleep; the soil of his homeland. The earth he would have rested in for eternity, if he had truly died, still had the power to bestow a little of that peace. It was a taste of that death, perhaps. It restored him. Without it he would waste away to nothing and become a shriveled thing, unable to move, unable to feed, but still unable to die. An undead hell.

He raised the painting to his lips and kissed it softly, then replaced it in the suitcase, closed the case, and flicked the catches shut. He needed rest but not the comalike trance that sometimes took him. He could always tell when that was coming. It took a big feed; a human feed. Now he just needed a dormant period to recharge, so to speak. He lifted the suitcase off the large desk and slid it into the cubbyhole beneath. He crawled in after it. He curled, encircling the case, and wrapped his arms around it, clutching it as if it were treasure.

He lay there, eyes open, staring beyond the room, beyond the school. Before he leapt into the dream, he thought of the girl again briefly. "Beautiful," he whispered. "Pale as the milk of death, thin and sharp like pain." And he drifted out to the stars.

·3·

Zoë

Zoë left the library early. It was no use sitting there doing nothing. She had stared at the wall, out the window, and at the clock; anything but write. Her fresh notebook page had become a mass of scribbled-out false starts. At this rate she would have nothing to show Mrs. Muir tomorrow in their critique session.

I want to write something beautiful about my mother, she thought. But it had all come out so trite, and she knew it. She wanted to write something important that spat in death's teeth. The trouble was, she didn't want Mrs. Muir to know about her mother. She didn't want her to say, "Poor thing," or something awful about God's will like that idiot woman next door, so what she ended up with was something less than honest, and dishonest poetry didn't work. But I can't write about anything else if I can't write about Mom, Zoë thought. She's the most important thing. God!

Zoë

I'm really blowing school. It was as close to being a perfect class as she could imagine, this independent-study business, yet if she continued like this it would be a waste of the quarter. I can't start screwing up in school, she thought. Mom has enough worries.

"Damn!" she muttered as she fumbled with her locker. It always stuck. She felt like kicking the stupid thing. Yet she just stood there glaring at it.

"It won't melt, no matter how long you stare at it," came a voice at her side.

"Lorraine! You snuck up quietly."

"You've got to sneak about when you cut as many classes as I do."

"Again?"

"Well, what's the use? I'm moving, aren't I? Right in the middle of the semester. And I'll start somewhere else right in the middle of their semester. I might as well give it up until after Christmas. Anyhow, it was worth it to see you use your X-ray vision."

Zoë smiled, yet was sad as she watched Lorraine work magic on the locker door. Who would make her laugh when Lorraine left? Who else would blithely ignore her requests for peace and quiet and drag her to a party anyway?

"Come to the bathroom with me," Lorraine said as Zoë stashed her books and got out her lunch. "It's between shifts, so we might even be able to breathe in there." They headed for the bathroom nearest the cafeteria. "I'm sorry

Zoë

about last night," Lorraine said as she barreled through the swinging doors of the bathroom.

"There's nothing to be sorry about," said Zoë behind her, surprised. Could she dare hope that Lorraine was ready to talk? They stood in front of the mirrors, and Lorraine pulled out a comb and tried to arrange her impossible auburn curls. "You'd think they'd replace these damn mirrors," she said angrily. "They're all cracked." Then she stopped the pretense of combing and turned to face Zoë, who saw her friend's face change suddenly. Uh-oh, Zoë thought.

"Zoë, I don't want to move," Lorraine barely got out before she started to cry fierce tears. "I won't have any friends. I'll have to start all over." Zoë's hopes plunged. She'd thought they were going to talk about her. It almost made her cry, too, but she held Lorraine, rubbed her back, and uttered an occasional "There, there." Inside, she was lost. How can I help you, she thought, when I can't even help myself? It was disturbing. Lorraine was the strong one. She didn't do this. The world was topsy-turvy again.

"I'm sorry," gasped Lorraine after a while. "I've no right to feel this way. I'm only moving. But you . . ." She sobbed again.

She can't say it, Zoë thought. We both know what she means, and she can't say it. It isn't your pity I want, she thought, and almost pushed her friend away, but stopped herself. Lorraine really did care. It wasn't her fault that people didn't know how to talk about death. Not Dad, not the neighbors, not Mom's friends. Death's partner was silence. Tenderness for her friend overwhelmed her dismay. "You nerd. You know you can always tell me how you feel. Usually nothing, including me, can stop you."

"But I feel so selfish."

You always are anyway, Zoë realized, but never on purpose. It was just the way Lorraine was. Zoë could almost take comfort in the familiarity of it. She gently shook her friend. "What will I do without you?"

That brought on more tears. "I'll miss you so much, Zoë."

They stood for a while, holding each other. It was rare that Lorraine let herself be fragile. After her mother left she was too afraid of breaking for good. At least that was what Zoë had guessed from watching her. We'll have another thing in common now, Zoë thought, but at least you'll be able to visit your mother. There was bitterness in this thought. She stroked Lorraine's hair in an attempt to atone. This was a moment when she could slip gently past Lorraine's guard. I'm afraid, too, she prepared to say. I'm afraid my mother will die, and my father will grieve forever, and I'll always be alone, because you're going too.

But there was a bell ringing somewhere, and second-period lunch was signaled. Damn, damn, damn, Zoë thought.

The door burst open, and a group of girls crowded in, already distributing cigarettes. Lorraine pushed Zoë away

Zoë

and hastily splashed water on her face. A blonde with garish makeup stood staring at them with her lit cigarette in a carefully poised hand.

"You guys queer or somethin'?" she asked jeeringly.

"Piss off, Morgan," said Lorraine, putting her arm around Zoë protectively. "You know, you could break your wrist holding a cigarette like that," and Zoë found herself being swept out of the bathroom. Things were back to normal.

In the cafeteria they sat at their usual table near the back door. "I'm going to get a death-burger," Lorraine said after checking her purse, and jumped up. "Hold the fort."

Zoë smiled with wry affection at Lorraine's tactlessness.

Just after Lorraine left, two girls Zoë recognized from physics class sat down at the other end of the table. They unwrapped sandwiches and chattered away between bites. Zoë felt a little guilty about listening, but it seemed imposssible not to, especially when they sat so near. She chased an idea for a poem around her head, something about a silver boy in the moonlight, but finally the word *murder* caught her attention and held it.

"She was Sheila's cousin," the dark one said dramatically as she leaned across the table.

"Really!"

"Yes, they found her with her throat slashed."

The tall one shuddered. "God, it's like Jack the Ripper or something."

"Ugh!" they agreed in unison.

Zoë

Lorraine returned with her lunch, and the other conversation faded into the background. "Have you been reading the paper lately?" Zoë asked Lorraine.

"Not really. Who's got time? Why?"

Zoë glanced at the girls at the end of the table, still engrossed in the details of murder. "Oh, there was something in the news. I saw a headline, but I didn't read about it. I thought you might know."

"Not me. They call me—Miss Oblivious," Lorraine camped in her Saturday-morning-cartoon voice.

Zoë laughed to cover her irritation. It was too true. "Never mind."

After school her father was outside to pick her up. "Hop in. We're going to the hospital," he said, but that was about all he said on the way. He concentrated on driving with the intensity of the newly licensed, as if one thing could block out all others. Zoë watched him carefully, waiting for news, but in vain. She wanted to say something, anything, to break the silence but couldn't think of an opening remark. Then they were there.

People always talked about hating the smell of hospitals. As they went up in the elevator, Zoë thought this one smelled rather pleasant, like evergreen or something. It was irritating that there should be anything to like. She worried a piece of paper in her coat pocket to shreds.

At the door she hesitated, afraid to go in. What does Mom look like this time? she wondered. Her father opened the door for her and she had to step inside. Zoë's throat seemed to close up when she saw her mother, a fragile stick-figure in the bed, with arms more bruised than ever from the needles and tubes.

"Mom?" she said in a slightly cracked voice.

Eyelashes fluttered, and her mother opened her eyes. She smiled weakly and her skin, dry as old parchment, crinkled with the effort. "Zoë," she whispered back in a voice just as cracked. "Darling." The bed whined as she moved it to a sitting position.

Zoë's gaze flicked around the room. She was repelled once more by the institutional-green walls, barely relieved by a drab forest scene, and a calendar that marked off the days for the record keepers. Her mother's name was in a slot above the bed, so each impersonal shift would know who she was. The medicine cabinet, cupboards, drawers, and counter were all painted white, and as easy to clean of stains as the pale tile floor. An unused television was tilted toward the window.

Her father nudged her forward. She started to sit, then wasn't sure. She glanced at him and he nodded, so she lowered herself into the chair at the bedside. Her father fussed around his wife, fluffing her pillow, straightening her sheets—all smiles, all teases. Where was the silent man who had driven here? Zoë wondered. When he was satisfied the patient was comfortable, he flopped into a chair on the other side of the room, giving them space to talk. He seemed to deflate when out of her mother's line of sight. He slouched, his hands dug deep into his tweed pockets, and glanced at Zoë with worried, unspoken questions. Zoë wished he'd ask them.

"A great view of the parking lot you've got," she said.

"I'm glad you like it." Zoë was shocked at how faint her mother's voice was despite the ironic tone.

Zoë reached for her hand and noticed a tightness around her eyes that she knew meant pain, as did the way her mother's other hand twisted a grasping of sheet. Zoë wanted to reach out and stop it. It hurt her to watch.

"Are you eating?" her mother asked.

"Are you?" Zoë shot back, glancing at the barely touched meal still sitting on the bedside tray.

"Touché."

"Come home soon, Mom. I miss you."

Zoë felt her hand squeezed gently. "I'll try, darling. I'll try."

Zoë's eyes filled with tears. Please don't cry, she begged herself. Don't upset her. "Guess what," she said, grabbing for anything. "The rose by the gate still has a bloom on it."

Her mother smiled. "Silly old thing. It doesn't seem decent at this time of year, does it?"

They were silent for a while. Zoë hated the way hospitals sucked everything you wanted to say right out of your head. It's bad enough that they leave the door open so the nurses can come and go, she thought, but then Dad sits there like some kind of guardian.

"I just needed to see you," her mother finally said.

Zoë

"Okay."

"You need to eat more, sweetheart. Wear some makeup."

Zoë laughed gently, and sniffed. "I remember when you would have taken a washcloth to me for wearing makeup, and now you're telling me to wear it. Do I look that bad?"

"Heavens, no. But you're old enough. You should get your hair cut in one of those new styles."

Zoë stroked a baby-fine tuft of her mother's newly grown hair. "Like you, huh?"

"Well, my punk look wasn't exactly intentional." She smiled. "And it looks a little pretentious on an old lady like me."

"But you're not old," Zoë said, her voice wavering.

"I'm thirsty," her mother said, still deft at diverting disaster. "Pour me a glass of water, please."

As Zoë reached for the pitcher, a nurse poked her head around the door. She nodded at Mr. Sutcliff, who then stepped forward. "That's enough for now," he said, holding Zoë's shoulders firmly, kissing the top of her head.

"Harry, no!" his wife protested, struggling to sit up in bed.

"You know what the doctor said," he answered, unyielding.

I'm being squeezed out again, Zoë thought bitterly, but she leaned and kissed the cheek offered to her.

"They totally ignore what I want around here," her mother said, as if apologizing.

28

Zoë

Outside the room her father tried to give Zoë cab fare, and some extra for dinner. She wanted to ignore it, but he closed her hand firmly around the bills with his large dry grip.

"What did the doctor say?" she asked point-blank.

His gaze shifted this way and that, as if he was afraid to look at her. "He says your visits tire your mother out. He doesn't want you visiting so much or for so long."

"Dad!" It came out as a howl.

"I'm sorry. The nurses have been alerted. Zay haf zer orders," he joked feebly.

"Don't you have any say?" she asked.

He finally looked her in the eyes. "Zoë, I think seeing you does your mother good, but he's the doctor. Let's try it his way for a while. I want what's best for her."

"So you're on his side—"

He cut off her protest with a gentle finger to her lips. "Get some pizza. Invite Lorraine over to keep you company," he said. "I'll stay for a bit longer." He stroked her cheek and left her in the hall.

What if I screamed and cried and made a fuss? she thought. What if I had a tantrum and begged them not to send me away? But she couldn't do that to them. She bit her lip and turned away.

Outside, she found one of the cabs that always lingered there. She rode home, worrying about how much to tip, so she wouldn't have to think about her mother, or another empty evening.

Zoë

She paid the cabdriver in front of her house, but when she got to the front door, she couldn't bring herself to fumble the key into the lock. She shoved it back into her jacket pocket. I can't face that silence right now, she thought. It's suffocating.

She went to the park and watched the children play until they were called away to dinner. It was company of sorts, yet undemanding. A few stragglers came back to defy the dusk curfew on the playground, but as the shadows became deeper, and the lights came on, even they were called back to warm beds in houses full of parents, brothers, sisters, and blaring TV sets.

I wish I had a brother or sister, she thought. Someone to take charge. I don't want to *have* to be responsible. I hate doing laundry. I hate having to remind Dad the phone bill's due. Mom always looked after us. The old anger rose. She thumped her knee gently with her fist as if to subdue it. She thought she'd gotten over that. It's not her fault, Zoë told herself. It's stupid to think that. She's not going away on purpose. But Dad's going to be a vegetable. Who's going to look after me?

A cold breeze swept through the park, and clouds blew across the early moon. Zoë pulled her denim jacket closer around her. It was time to get the heavier coats out from the storage closet upstairs. She shivered suddenly, as if ice trickled down her spine.

"It's a beautiful night," came a soft voice beside her.

She turned swiftly, heart pounding. A young man sat

there. The lamplight outlined him against the dark bushes behind like a ring of frost around the moon. He smiled at her as a cat smiles, with secret humor. "You scared me," she whispered fiercely. Who was this person invading her bench?

"I'm sorry," he said, but he didn't look it.

She recognized him then, from last night. As if he saw this he said, "We're even now. You scared me."

"Why should you be scared?" she demanded. "It's you creeping up on people."

"Why should you be?" he asked.

Zoë bristled defensively. "I don't like evasive conversation."

"Do you like any conversation?"

"No. I want to be alone."

"I think you are alone." He reached for her hand. She snatched it away and stood up. How dare he be right, then take advantage of it? He seemed surprised for a second, but then his smile deepened, and a dreamy look was on his face. "Please stay," he said in tones soft as a lullaby. His eyes were huge, dark, and gentle. She hesitated for a moment. He seemed so understanding. Surely she could talk to him. Then her anger surfaced again. The manipulative jerk, she thought.

"I don't know what you're after," she said, "but you can look for it somewhere else." She turned and walked firmly away.

"It strikes me," he called after her in a voice now with

an edge to it, "that girls who sit alone in parks at night are the ones after something."

She was so furious, she could have screamed. She almost turned, but no, she thought, that's what he wants. She walked on. Her anger carried her home before she knew it. Strangely, it had made her hungry. She ate better than she had in weeks.

She hesitated once between mouthfuls with a feeling of dread. Was he weird? Would he have hurt her? No. He looked like an angel in a Renaissance painting. Could beauty hurt?

· 4 ·

Simon

Simon watched the girl walk away, a cloud of anger around her. He was bemused. She had not responded correctly. He had started to moon-weave, and she had broken it. She had snapped it with anger. He was interested. He followed her.

He slipped gradually into a half state, nearer mist than form. It was easy—like dreaming, really—just let go of body and drift. His consciousness held molecules together with tendrils of thought. He blended with the shadows and became the air. She would never see. He flowed beneath trees, slid along walls, cut corners through dying autumn flowers. He always kept her in sight. She walked fast, shimmering the crisp air with her breath.

They usually came to him when his eyes softened with the moon, when he crushed his voice like velvet. They let him caress them. They tipped their heads back and drowned in the stars, while he stroked exposed throat and wallowed in conquest. Sometimes he let them go and allowed them to think it a dream. He left before they broke the spell of his eyes, to sit blinking and head-shaking in cold predawn wind. Sometimes the dark hunger awoke too strong to hold. He clenched them tight, sank fangs deep into yielding neck, and fed on the thick, hot soup of their life. He was lost in the throbbing ecstasy song of blood pumping, life spurting, until blood, horror, and life ebbed, and he abandoned the limp remnants to seek dark sleep.

He stood at the wooden gate, watching the girl enter a forest-green door with diamond windows. He trembled with desire. Lights came on in the house. He circled it, peering in windows—a peeping Tom, ecstasy denied. He inhaled details from the golden warmth he could never have: an Oriental carpet, an antique armoire, cream kitchen tiles, and a painting of bright, crazed, laughing girls. His eyes narrowed. The girls in the painting looked right at him. Just a painting, he chided, but he felt mocked, and an anger rumbled deep in his throat. The lights downstairs dimmed. A light came on above. She goes to sleep, he thought, and begrudged her rest when he had none.

He paced her garden with slinking gait, examining basement windows and garage doors. He could not enter unless invited, but he liked to know the ways in, and out, if needed. The animal was close to the surface tonight. It reminded him of when he first changed, when he roamed the woods like a beast for what seemed an eternity, mindless from shock. Threads of memory clung to him, though most was a blur. Images sparked bright at times; pictures frozen in the muted green light of the forest—savaged corpses of animals, or a gamekeeper crumpled and drained amid the fallen leaves, his head barely attached to his neck. Simon could not ever control it then, and his attack was fierce, made vicious by his own fear. It took a long time to regain the capacity to think. It took longer to leave the forest. But the forest had never left him. Tonight it echoed in him like owl cries, and pine needles rustling.

He marked his territory like a wolf, and urinated on the back-door steps. It helped a little. I know where you live, he thought.

He walked then. He walked long and far, beating the anger beneath his feet. The quiet, dream-laden suburbs gave way to the street life of the urban fringe. Here the streets pulsed with light from corner bars and pizza palaces, late-night video-game arcades, and record stores that seemed to never close. The hot boys stood on street corners, whispering promises of romance to girls in leather skirts who knew that they were lies. Groups of lonely people huddled together against the dark. He felt a kinship here. He was as separate as they amid the crowd. No one saw him. He was too much like the undernourished,

Simon

ill-clad street waifs of this jangling street to catch an eye. A group of boys ran laughing down the sidewalk, one waving a shirt above his head, bare-chest drunk. Girls paraded bargain-store fashions, their bleached hair and bedroom eyes hiding the fear that they weren't good enough. Soon the cold would force them inside, so they clutched at lost summer.

Simon drifted off the main road to the darker streets. He hummed pitch perfect a song he had gathered along the way. It was one of the angry songs he enjoyed. He beat out its driving rhythm on his thigh as he walked. Occasionally he'd sing a phrase, when he remembered the words.

He paced the uneven pavement in front of row houses with peeling paint but well-scrubbed steps. Through one uncurtained window at a corner house he saw a woman on a man's lap in a shabby chair. They were laughing at a game show on TV. He could have stood there unnoticed for an hour. Suddenly he wanted to smash the window and scream, "Look at me!" He wanted to be noticed. He wanted people to see him. It was dangerous, this want. It was mad. But sometimes he was afraid that he didn't exist. Now and again someone recognized what he was. They had to die. If they didn't, well . . . It was foolish not to think of protecting himself. There was no one who knew him, no one to say his name.

He turned a corner and startled a dog. They cringed and

growled at each other. The dog's hackles spiked, then it whimpered and ran. Simon walked on and found a weed-choked vacant lot. Its only inhabitant was an abandoned car. He sat on a ruined wall and gazed at the moon.

"Hey, boy!" A call from the high brick wall next door. A leg was flung over, and then a scruffy youth of about sixteen pulled himself astride it.

Boy, Simon thought sarcastically. He smiled in anticipation.

"Yeah, you!" came a deeper voice. Another youth, perhaps a touch older, stepped out from behind the car. He was a big lout in jeans and a flannel shirt like a lumberjack.

A sneering boy in a leather jacket followed him. "This is our lot," he hissed. He carried a half-empty liquor bottle and swayed slightly. His right hand flashed silver. Simon saw he carried a knife. Simon didn't like long pointy things. They made him nervous. He didn't like being nervous.

A scuffling announced the descent of the wall straddler, a thud his landing. The boys spread out and converged on Simon. He rose slowly from his perch, muscles tightened. The boys advanced.

"Where you from?"

"You ain't from here."

"Nobody here knows you."

Simon

"Yeah," spoke the wall climber. "And if nobody knows you, you ain't nobody." He giggled, a high-pitched, nervous sound, and wiped his hands against a ragged Ozzie Osbourne T-shirt.

Nobody. Even this scum called him nobody. Simon stepped toward the danger, into their net. They'd caught shark this time. He smiled.

"Pretty tough, huh?" said the big one mockingly.

The boy with the leather jacket settled his bottle into the crotch of two bricks. "Pretty stupid, you mean." He tossed his knife from hand to hand. "You a retard or somethin'?"

"Yeah. He's too dumb to be scared."

Simon turned his back on the third boy, the one who had said that. He was a sheep. The big one was a bully, but the leather-clad one was trouble. He was crazy. He didn't smoke weed, he smoked green. Simon could smell it on him. It reeked like burning plastic and it killed the brain. It made people think they couldn't die.

"This is our playground, buddy."

"Yeah, wanna play?"

Simon finally spoke. "Is that what you said to your mother last night?"

"Son of a . . ." The big one charged him, swinging meaty fists.

Simon stepped aside, quick as thought. The boy stumbled, looked confused, then turned like an angry bear to attack again. Simon stepped aside once more. His opponent breathed heavily. Simon smiled. Get the biggest one, and the rest often run. But he kept the crazy one in his sight all the same. You didn't know about dusters.

They danced a lopsided waltz on the waste ground, and the big youth's fury grew and grew. Then Simon stood still. The boy grabbed. He expected to miss but, to his surprise, found that the quarry was his. He panted and grinned. He had Simon's arm in a crushing hold, as he prepared a blow. And Simon, who didn't come up to his chin, clutched the boy's belt with his free hand and lifted him into the air. The boy waved his arms like an insect and gurgled with fear. The boy in the jacket spat an oath but was frozen, enthralled. The other boy trembled but couldn't move either. Simon threw his opponent then, an impossible distance. The boy sailed the air for a moment, then crashed in a pile of debris. The sound broke the spell, and Simon heard the third boy run.

But the boy with the knife laughed. He slinked forward, steel flickering in the streetlight. He had seen a fight or two, Simon surmised, but probably won through sheer viciousness, not skill. Best to deal with him as a cat does a rat—no play, snap it fast.

The boy was expecting another dance, not for his victim to walk right up to him. He hesitated a second, confronted with craziness greater than his, then he saw something in

Simon's eyes that made him lunge. He slashed wildly in fear, but too late. His knife went flying. His arm, captured for a moment, went limp, and searing, and useless. He backed away.

It was Simon's turn to laugh; a sound dark and cursed. The blow he landed snapped the boy back and smashed him against the car. The boy started to slide to the ground, but slim white hands reached for him delicately and slammed him once more against the car. The third blow rendered him unconscious and flooded Simon with the sweet warm pleasure of the kill.

"Call me nobody?" he whispered, and his fangs slid from their sheaths. "Call me nobody?" he screamed as if in pain. He hoisted his victim up and tore the boy's wrist open with a savage scissoring of teeth. He raised the boy's arm and, with the pulsing blood, wrote wavering letters on the dingy primer of the car's roof. I AM.

The dark, raw smell of blood intoxicated. He found himself embracing the boy and pulling the damaged wrist up to his mouth. Faintly, somewhere, he felt disgust. A distant echo cried for him to stop. But the blood call was too strong. He had almost placed a reverent kiss upon the hand when sirens screamed too close.

He pushed the limp body from him, but it seemed to cling. For a moment he felt trapped. Then it slid to the ground. But in the midst of panic a perverse whim took hold. He began to strip the jacket from the huddled form, struggling with the boy's inert bulk, bloodying the lining, ripping a seam until it pulled free. Black and glittering, he had his prize. He clutched it to him, leaving its owner his life.

Then he was running. He fled past his first assailant, now staring with white-faced rictus fear, though the rubble of lost homes, out into the night, on and on through the streets, until he arrived in the quiet yard of a house with a dark green door.

He wrapped the bloodstained jacket about his shoulders and sank down beneath an azalea bush. He stared at her window until dawn.

· 5 ·

Zoë

Zoë froze in the doorway, her clenched fist to her mouth. Her teeth dug into her knuckles. Anne Sutcliff sprawled over the side of the chaotic hospital bed. Her shoulders heaved. The sounds were unmistakable.

"Dad." Zoë turned and clutched her father's arm. "She's throwing up." The disrupted IV regulator beeped furiously.

Mom's friend Carol, who'd come with them, squeezed Zoë's shoulder. "Don't worry, hon. I'll get a nurse."

Zoë's father pushed by her and raced the few strides that took him to his wife's side. "It's all right, baby. It's all right." He smoothed back the hair from her face rhythmically.

"I'm sorry," she moaned between retches.

When her father reached impatiently for a button at the bedside, Zoë saw that a few strands of dark hair still clung to his fingers. He shook them into the trash can, which was half full with needle covers and stained gauze.

42

Zoë

The smell of the room was overpowering. She backed out of the door, the bile rising in her own throat. Her heart pounded. She wanted to run to her mother, but she couldn't bear to stay and see her that way. Mothers are supposed to be strong, she thought. She's supposed to take care of me.

A nurse bustled by her.

Zoë knew the treatment made her mother sick, but she'd never seen her this bad, so weak she couldn't even make it to the bathroom. Zoë felt awful, embarrassed, like she was spying on something private.

Carol tried to put an arm around her, but Zoë shook her off.

I should go to Mom, Zoë told herself. She needs me. But she couldn't go back into the room and face that sick woman. She leaned against the wall of the corridor in a cold sweat, shaking. Carol hovered close by, looking hurt and anxious.

This is stupid, Zoë thought. You wanted to help, to prove you belonged. Here's your chance. Her mind argued logically, but her body refused to move. Finally, she began to edge toward the door. I could hold her hand, at least, she thought, and comfort her. I owe it to her.

But before she got there, her father came back out. He put his arms around her. "She's a bit better now," he said. "She might be able to sleep." He sounded drained. She hugged back, relieved that the decision had been taken away from her, hungry for comfort, but he pulled away too fast.

Zoë

"Come on," he said. "I'll drive you both home."

"I'll stay, Harry," Carol said. "I want to stay." She smiled tentatively at Zoë. "Zoë, hon. Call me, okay? If you need something. You know you can."

Zoë nodded vaguely—Carol meant to be kind—then followed her father, eager to get away, and ashamed of it.

On the silent trip in the car she began to feel guilty. I could have helped her, she thought. He didn't give me a chance to get myself together.

"Are you going back?" she asked.

He nodded.

"I thought so." It was like he wanted to keep her all to himself. Carol got to stay. She slouched in the seat beside him and dug her hands deep into her pockets. I'm sulking, she thought. Then, I don't care. But she was being silly, and she knew it. He'd always been a wonderful dad, and he loved her too. But we never do anything together now, she thought, not even be unhappy together. He makes decisions without asking me, like I'm a little child.

Her hand found a small object in her pocket. She had discovered it on the back steps this morning when she took the garbage out, lying there spiky and shiny. Zoë the bird, the magpie, had picked it up, attracted by its sparkle. But she was late for school, and had shoved it into her coat pocket while she ran to gather her books, then forgotten it. She pulled it out to look at it again, rolling it between her fingers. Little points jabbed her. It looked like a star, a sort of stud. Funny how things get around, she thought.

Zoë

Go on, ask me what it is, she dared her dad silently, but he didn't notice, so she shoved it back into her pocket.

"Drop me at Lorraine's, please," she asked as they pulled into the neighborhood. She tossed her notebook into the backseat before she got out of the car. She hadn't even had a chance to read anything to her mother today, and her mother was her truest critic. "I'll get it later," she said. "Bye." He smiled vaguely and pulled away, his mind already back at the hospital.

Lorraine looked pleased to see Zoë. "Hi, Zo. Just in time. I was thinking of going out."

Lorraine will understand, she thought, and that triggered the tears, because she wasn't sure. She collapsed on the couch, and Lorraine crouched in front of her, one hand lightly on Zoë's knee, waiting for her to stop crying. Zoë pulled herself together. "I'm sorry," she said. "I couldn't help it." She told Lorraine what had happened at the hospital, briefly, simply. She didn't mention the embarrassment, or the shame of not being able to respond.

Lorraine squeezed her knee. "You'll go again. It'll be better next time."

"Yeah." Zoë wiped her eyes with an offered tissue. "I'm such a wimp," she said. "I always seem to be crying."

Lorraine smiled and punched Zoë's shoulder gently. "Listen, Dad sent me some guilt money. He said to buy some clothes to impress my new friends with when I get out there." She made a face. "Want to go shopping?"

Zoë

"I'm not sure."

"Oh, come on. You deserve an outing."

Zoë swept the hair from her face with short, tense movements as she thought about it.

"Well, I've got to get out anyway, before Diane comes back," Lorraine continued. "She's pissed she didn't get any money. She was clomping around like a madwoman all morning. Please, please, please!"

"All right," Zoë said, and stopped frowning. She felt a little uneasy, though. It didn't seem right to go shopping, as if everything were normal.

Lorraine got her jacket, and they left. "Pity you didn't know we were going shopping—you could have asked your dad for money too."

"No money for clothes right now," Zoë said, trying to sound matter-of-fact. "Too many bills."

"God, at least a decent pair of pants," Lorraine said. "Hey, slow down."

Zoë lessened her pace and took a deep breath. Come on, she told herself, lighten up.

"There's nothing wrong with plain old Levi's," she said, poking Lorraine, inviting play.

Lorraine grinned, invitation accepted, but when Zoë turned the corner to go to the Center, Lorraine held back. "Not there," Lorraine called after her. "Let's be hedonistic and go to the mall." She led the way to the bus stop. "I've got to be back by seven, though. I've got a date with Neil."

Zoë

"Oh, gross," Zoë said, teasing her.

Lorraine squealed in outrage right on cue.

They squabbled playfully until the bus came.

They arrived at the mall, their plan of action already mapped out. "New jeans, a few shirts, and a pair of shoes," Lorraine had finally decided. She marched Zoë right away to the Jean Jar, then Muggles, through Finders, and on to the Edge. On the way they picked up a couple of oversized, bright sweatshirts, and an expensive cotton shirt emblazoned with one of the new fall designs. It took a lot of trying on, but Lorraine managed to find a pair of pants she liked as well. "Too good for mere mortals," she gloated, looking at herself in the dressing-room mirror.

At first it seemed remote to Zoë, as if she were an observer from another planet, but Lorraine's enthusiasm was hard to resist. Despite the occasional hesitation Zoë found she was getting into the spirit of things. "Let's go to that punk store down the other end," she said, knowing that would entice her friend.

"I don't know, dahling," Lorraine gushed. "I already have leopard-skin pants, shoes, shirts, underwear, and sanitary napkins."

They went anyhow, and laughed with pleasure at the T-shirt designs, and dared each other to buy colored hairspray. "It washes out," Lorraine whispered. "Come on. You'd look great with a purple streak."

"No one wears that anymore," Zoë said. "I'd rather have a T-shirt that says EAT THE RICH." She tried not to laugh too loud and offend the clerks, who all seemed to take their black, spiky selves very seriously.

"Here, I'll buy you a going-away present," Lorraine said.

Zoë's stomach turned over. "I'd rather you didn't."

"Don't be silly," Lorraine said. "You have a choice between the T-shirt or this necklace here." She pointed to an exquisite little silver crucifix on a deep red ribbon.

How can you talk about it so casually? Zoë thought. You said you didn't want to go, now you're buying me good-bye presents. How can you change so fast? "It seems so out of place here," she said aloud.

"Not if you look at the people working here. They're dripping with them. It all depends on the way you wear it."

"I like the ribbon, but it seems like a weird combination somehow. My grandmother would have a fit."

"Considering she lives in Europe, I doubt if she'll see it much."

Lorraine went to the cash register and bought the necklace, plus some green hair-dye for herself. "What the hell," she said. "I can always threaten to show up at a business lunch wearing it, if Dad needs keeping in line."

Outside she jabbed a camouflage-patterned box at Zoë. "Here." For once she seemed awkward.

Zoë slipped it into her jacket pocket, blushing. Lorraine didn't have to get her a present to be remembered. I won't wear it, she thought. I don't like it.

Zoë

"Shoes!" Lorraine screamed like a war cry, causing several passersby to turn and stare. What a subtle way of avoiding sentiment, Zoë thought with wry amusement.

Lorraine launched into a monologue as they headed for the nearest shoe store. "I love shoe shopping, especially if it's a salesman. They grovel at your feet, and run and fetch, and put them on for you. God, it gives me a feeling of power."

After the final purchase they had pizza at the Roma. They recognized some kids from school there.

"Peter Ziegler," Lorraine moaned. "I hope I don't get something stuck between my teeth."

Zoë chuckled. "I don't think it matters, since he probably won't come over here anyway."

"Killjoy. Hey, he's with that Keith whatzisname you went out with last spring. What was wrong with him? I can't remember."

Zoë sighed. "Nothing was wrong with him. I don't know. I guess I just wasn't attracted to him."

"When will you be attracted, Zo, for goodness' sake? I mean, my God, you're almost seventeen."

"I know, I know." Zoë pushed a pizza crust around her plate, annoyed at having to go through this again. Lorraine seemed to think that everyone should have hyperactive hormones like her.

"Sorry, I've pissed you off, haven't I? I'll back off."

Zoë had to admit it was a rare perceptive moment on Lorraine's part. The girls' eyes met then in an unspoken

Zoë

peace agreement, and they ate for a while in companionable silence.

Boys, Zoë thought. Why aren't I as loony about them as Lorraine? I guess people are different. She smiled at how ludicrously obvious that statement was. But they seem to like me, so I suppose I'm not gross or anything, she decided. She remembered suddenly the pale boy in the park—a surprisingly clear glimpse of him, sparklingly sharp in the moonlight. She tried to dismiss her excitement with anger. I guess I was supposed to be flattered.

"Let's see a movie," Lorraine said, brushing the crumbs from around her mouth. "They've got an el cheapo horror twilight show at the Cinema Three. None left alive for two twenty-five."

"I'd rather not," Zoë said a little too fast. She saw Lorraine cringe at her mistake. Feeling sorry for her, she added, "There's a new French movie there, too, that everyone's been talking about. Perhaps we could see that."

Lorraine relaxed. "I try *not* to talk about things like that. Anyway, whenever I see a movie with subtitles, I come out expecting to see them in real life for an hour or two. It's weird."

"What's the other one?"

"Oh, something based on a Saturday-morning cartoon."

"Yuck!"

"No kidding!"

They decided to forget about a movie and take the bus back to Oakwood. Zoë was relieved. She didn't think she

Zoë

could sit through a movie, no matter how entertaining. By the time they got off the bus at Oakwood Village the daylight had fled, and the streetlights come on. As the world became darker, so did Zoë's mood. How could I go out and enjoy myself? she thought.

As if she had read Zoë's thoughts, Lorraine tugged at her arm briefly. "Hey, it was good, right? You needed a break."

"Yeah." Zoë had to admit that she'd needed it, but now she should get back to the house. Perhaps she'd missed a vital phone call while she was out. However, now that she was near, she dreaded going home; she dreaded the news a phone call might bring.

"Earth to Zoë! Come in, please."

Zoë looked up with a start.

"I was saying," Lorraine continued, "I have to run into the drugstore."

"Oh, I'll wait here, then," Zoë said, stopping outside the bookstore. "They've got a new display."

"Okay."

Lorraine trotted up the sidewalk to the drugstore on the other side of the alley that divided the row of shops into two sections. There were fewer people on the street now. Everyone was going home for dinner. The autumn wind was picking up, and Zoë thought she felt a drop of rain on her cheek. There was a hint of woodsmoke in the air. It always made her feel vaguely lonely to smell someone's cozy fire when she was out in the night.

Zoë

She examined the contents of the window. She loved bookstores: they were an addiction. Even books she would never read held a fascination when arranged in a bright display. A book called *The Secret Life of Vegetables* caught her eye. It made her unbearably curious. She was wondering if it was about recent botanical discoveries, or a kinky sex novel, when she heard Lorraine's voice.

She looked up to see her friend talking to a small pale child with white hair who stood at the alley mouth. From his left hand dangled a shabby teddy bear. He looked fragile. He must only be about six, Zoë thought. What's he doing here alone at this time? She walked to join them. The child said something. Lorraine held out her hand, and he gave her a dazzling smile. Then he saw Zoë. The smile faded.

"S'all right," he said in a piping voice. "I 'member now." And he took off running down the street toward Chestnut.

"Appealing little monster," said Lorraine, although she looked puzzled. "Said he was lost. Albino, I think. He wanted me to help him find his mother down there." She pointed down the alley.

Zoë peered into the dark. "Why would she be down there?"

Lorraine shrugged. "Beats me. I almost felt like humoring him, though." She stared gloomily through the bookstore window. "Yuck! Hey, that reminds me, Dad sent me a reading list from this school I'm supposed to be going to.

Great, huh?'' She rolled her eyes. "It's supposed to help me fit in. I wonder what it'll be like.''

Zoë tensed. "Listen, why don't you go on home? The bookstore's open late tonight. I want to browse for a while.'' She was appalled to hear the words come out stiff and remote.

Lorraine glanced sharply at Zoë, but her voice remained neutral. "Bookstores make me break out.''

"I know.'' Zoë's tone was carefully gentler. "So go on. You've got to get ready for Naughty Neil.''

Lorraine took the cue. "Well, okay. I'll call you tomorrow and tell you the juicy details.''

"Spare me.''

"It's the only way you'll find out anything at this rate,'' Lorraine yelled over her shoulder as she took off for home.

Zoë waved her on with mock impatience. "Get outta here.'' Her voice was meant to sound jolly but, I don't want to hear about your shitty new school, she thought. I don't want to hear about your stupid date, and I don't want to go home.

It won't work. It's not magic, Zoë told herself as she entered the store. Just 'cause you're not there to hear of it, doesn't mean it can't happen. Nevertheless, it felt better to put off going home for now. She headed straight for the window display, but the intriguing title turned out to be merely a cookbook. She looked around for half an hour anyhow, until screaming sirens pulling up outside brought her and the other browsers to the front of the store.

Zoë

She panicked for a moment. Lorraine. But, of course, Lorraine was long gone. How Zoë hated sirens. They howled to the scene of an emergency like ravenous banshees and left behind emptiness.

A bald man came pushing into the store, white-faced, babbling with shock. "They found a body in the alley. Briggs at the pharmacy found it," he announced to no one in particular.

The smart blond woman who ran the bookstore sat down heavily in her seat behind the sales counter. "What?"

"Briggs was leaving work," the man continued. "He had his bicycle in the alley. He almost fell over the woman. Her throat is slashed."

People looked at each other, dumbfounded. "Another one," someone whispered. Zoë remembered seeing the bald man stocking shelves at the grocery store.

More people gathered outside—late shoppers, people going home, others going out for the night. Drawn like flies to blood, Zoë thought, and shuddered. She had to get home.

She squeezed past the bald man and went out the door. The bell above the door rang with cheery dissonance. A couple moved to let her out. She found herself next to a hastily erected police barrier, just in time to see something under a sheet being loaded into an ambulance.

"Must have happened recently," she heard a woman say in hushed tones.

She felt hot and ill. "Excuse me. Excuse me." She had

to get home. She navigated the crush of the still-forming crowd on the narrow sidewalk. "Excuse me. Excuse me." Where did they come from? Flies. She was sweating. She felt trapped. People jostled to keep their vantage point as she tried to get by.

Then she was past them into the night, leaning against the window of the grocery store, eyes closed, gasping deep, ragged breaths.

And a cold, soothing hand was stroking her forehead, cooling, comforting.

"It's death," came a whisper.

Her eyes shot open.

55

· 6 ·

Simon

He saw the dark-haired girl push herself from the crowd as if drowning, and lean against the shopwindow, gasping for air. He went to her helplessly, drawn by her fear. He couldn't help but touch her to taste it.

"It's death," he told her, wanting to explain.

Her eyes burst open, pinning him with a stricken look.

"It's death that frightens you so."

He felt slightly afraid himself now. This was the second time her eyes had held him. Combined with the enticing smell of fear, it was almost more than he could bear.

"Yes," she said, blinking, relaxing, breaking the spell.

His hand left her and fell to twist nervously at a shiny stud on his leather jacket. "I'm sorry. I'm always startling you." He didn't want to break the connection, not yet. It unnerved him when her eyes caught him like that, but it brought something else he couldn't explain, something that didn't seem normal for him. He wanted it again. He wanted to discover what it was.

"How did you know? About death, I mean." She had accepted his apology.

"I've seen its effect on people before now."

Her eyes grew troubled on his behalf, as she guessed wildly at his tragedy. It was so easy, Simon thought. He could tell the truth and let her lie for him. She would be too polite to ask outright. She would make it what she wanted it to be. The time was right. She needed to jump to another person, away from her fear. But why did he care so much? She had warm, rich blood, but it wasn't only that. Was it?

"I'm sorry," she said. "I haven't been too pleasant either." She smiled faintly. At herself, he guessed.

"You look shaken. Can I walk you home?" He started to offer his arm, then remembered it was an outdated custom and stopped.

She debated with herself. He saw the brief inward look. "Please," she said. He had passed the test.

They left the stores and walked slowly, quiet at first. He enjoyed her next to him. "You are late for dinner," he said finally.

"No. No one's home."

He saw that she immediately regretted having said that. Her lips tightened for a moment. She's calling herself a fool, he thought. It's not a thing to admit to a stranger. Reassure. "What a shame. This is the kind of night one likes to go home to a hot meal.'' He saw her lips quiver with unbidden amusement. ''I said something funny?''

She smiled fully now. ''I'm sorry, but you don't look . . . I mean . . . well, the way you talk. It's not how I would expect someone in a leather jacket to talk.''

Had he made a mistake? He didn't talk much to people. They were a temptation. They were food. One did not talk to food, or learn its speech patterns. It all changed so fast while he remained the same, watching it go by in flashing colors between the night. No. She was smiling. Somehow it pleased her, this discrepancy. It made her feel more at ease.

''It was a whim,'' he said, stroking the leather.

''It looks good on you.''

She wishes not to offend me, he thought. He was happy with that. How silly that it made him happy.

''Do you live near here?'' she asked.

''Close.''

''Yes?''

''It's temporary.''

''Are your parents looking for a permanent home in Oakwood?''

''My parents are dead.''

She looked aghast at her faux pas. Her hand rose partially to her mouth.

''It's all right. I've been alone a long time.'' He took her hand and lowered it gently. She was alone, too, he guessed, that was why she cared so much. Her hand was

soft and thin; it prickled him sweetly. She tugged her hand
back, and he knew she had felt it too. He disengaged. He
would not press.

She was quiet again. They walked. Once she looked as
if she were almost ready to speak, ready to tell him something, but she changed her mind. He wished she had told
him, because he wanted to hear her talk. He wanted to
know about her. This is not my nature, he thought. This is
not the beast. But, for that moment, he felt as if the beast
were unraveling from him in a fresh wind. He was thinking of questions to entice her to speak when they reached
her gate. He held it open for her, feeling disappointed that
the walk was over.

She stopped at the front door and turned to face him
firmly. Simon got the message. This is as far as I get. "I
hope you feel better soon," he said, acknowledging the
barrier.

Her stance relaxed as she felt his compliance. "Thank
you for walking me home. It shook me up, seeing that. I
expect we'll read about it tomorrow."

"Yes."

"My name's Zoë," she said, almost as an afterthought.

"Zoë," he repeated softly, like distant bees.

"What's yours?"

He looked at her and, trapped in her eyes again, felt
impelled, but his name caught in his throat. He had not
told it in so long that it felt too intimate to reveal it, like

giving away a portion of his true self. Yet her eyes were intimate also, stealing into him, opening locked doors.

He breathed his name. "Simon."

"Good night, Simon," she said gently, and turned.

He reached for her urgently, "Wait."

She halted and glanced back, worry flickering in her features.

He calmed himself. "If I come to see you here, will you invite me in?"

She gazed at him a moment, assessing him. "Yes, I think so."

He could smile now, and perhaps that was why she still hesitated. She was very close. He leaned closer, mouth parted to inhale the scent of her. Was it dark veins that called to him, or her soft lips? He didn't know. It made him dizzy. She almost swayed to meet him, her eyes drowning him, but she blushed and turned to the door again.

"Good night."

"Until next time," he whispered as she closed the door.

Walking back to the shops, he saw the boy with his mother. They had stopped so that she could adjust the scarf around his neck. I'd like to tighten it, Simon thought, and slipped into the shadows.

"Christopher," the mother said, "you've been to the store several times now. I don't see how you could get lost. When I saw all those policemen, I was really worried. Please don't wander off like that."

Simon

They began to walk again, and Simon followed. The child looked around as if he felt something. Simon let more distance come between them.

"We'll have to bundle you up better tomorrow, when we go to school. That was a nasty burn. Your poor skin. It's so delicate."

The boy didn't seem to be paying any attention to her, but looked all around him as if seeking something.

"That was a long nap you took today," the woman continued. "Mrs. Cohen said she could hardly wake you. What a sleepyhead you are. You should sleep at night, like a good boy. Maybe some hot milk will help tonight."

The child grimaced. The first sign that he had heard. They turned the corner.

"I've bought some yummy liver for dinner. You like that, don't you?"

Simon let them go. The boy was well occupied now. He would check again later.

Simon wandered the streets. He looked in at the all-night Laundromat, but it was deserted. Eventually he went to the 7-Eleven. He sat on a wall outside and watched the people come and go.

Teenagers screamed up in worn but well-loved cars, to grab a six-pack and a package of Marlboros. A husband hurried in for next morning's milk and left with a *Playboy* carefully secreted under his overcoat. Young men discussed The Game, in the light of windows plastered with signs touting ninety-nine-cent hot dogs, then slid off into the night in new machines. A drunk argued over the change from his five-dollar bill, mistaken lout. A girl pleaded with someone at the pay phone outside and stamped her feet either with cold or frustration, he couldn't tell.

He made up stories about them—what he might say to them if he deigned to talk, where they might go. The multicolored, overpriced stock became the scenery on his stage, and he was the only audience.

Sometimes he drifted in and out of now, reminded of previous stories he had seen or been a part of. On one such time, drifting into focus again, he saw the back of a girl with long dark hair at the counter. Zoë, he thought hopefully. But she turned, and it wasn't her.

When she left, he followed her anyway, out into the night. Nowhere else to go.

· 7 ·

Zoë

Zoë was awakened by the phone ringing. It went on and on. When her father didn't answer, she got up groggily and made her way to her parents' bedroom. The door was open and the bed unmade. She picked up the phone. It was her father, and she was momentarily confused. Then she remembered with the rush of full awakening. He had been called away, late last night, to the hospital.

"Hi, Zo," he said. "You did get back to sleep, then?"

"Yes." She flushed guiltily at having to answer that way.

"Mom's not too good, I'm afraid. I'm going to stay here, but don't you come down, okay? There's nothing you can do right now. Listen, I'll call you after school, or this evening, and let you know how she is."

He thinks I'm useless, she thought, because I froze when Mom was sick. "Will she be all right?"

63

"Yeah, she'll be fine."

Liar, she thought. "Are you coming home later?"

"Maybe not. I'll let you know."

"Dad, if she's feeling better tomorrow—"

"I don't think I can talk about that right now. One thing at a time. Okay?"

There was always an excuse to keep her away. "Okay," Zoë muttered. Left out again. She clenched the phone tight.

"There's a good girl. Take care."

"Bye," she said, and the phone clicked off. She slammed the receiver down.

In the quiet she heard her clock-radio's alarm going off in her room. It was too late to go back to bed now; she had to get ready for school. She went to shut off the awful music.

Zoë was looking under the couch for her shoes when the phone rang again. She snatched it up. Had her father changed his mind? But it was Pat Reynolds, the owner of the gallery her mother showed at.

"We're having an opening tomorrow night," she said. "I thought you might like to come. I mean, I know Harry's busy. I thought you might like to get out."

"I don't know, Pat," Zoë said. "I'd feel out of place without Mom."

"There'll be people you know there."

But they'd all be her parents' friends. They would greet her with overly jolly hellos and then not know what to say next. She hated those awkward silences. She'd be miserable. "Can I think about it?"

"Sure, Zoë, call me. Take care." They both knew she wouldn't come.

She left early, to avoid more phone calls, although maybe that was a mistake. Usually the walk to school meant a welcome chance to think, but today she didn't want to think. It would be all right if Lorraine were there. Lorraine could make her feel better. But Lorraine had driver's ed at eight o'clock, and had left an hour ago. It was the only course she showed up for consistently.

The rhythm of Zoë's steps reminded her of another walk. Who was that boy, Simon? Was he a runaway, or what? He wasn't from around there, because he seemed to have a slight accent of some sort. He was so matter-of-fact about his parents being dead. Was he lying, she wondered, or was it so long ago it was like an old wound—only aching sometimes? Could you get used to it? If so, maybe he had something to teach her about survival. She couldn't figure him out. One minute he was nervous, and the next he seemed so confident. It was funny, she had thought she was leading him, but now that she looked back on it, she realized he had never hesitated once, as if he knew the way. Silly, she thought. He couldn't have.

Zoë kept her eyes on the moss-bordered flagstones of the sidewalk as she walked, glancing up to avoid the occasional pedestrian, or to cross an intersection. Step on a crack; break your mother's back, she thought, remembering childhood magic. Then, irrationally, she was stepping into the middle of each paving stone, avoiding the grooves between them, trying to coordinate her steps at an even pace to miss the cracks. She had to hop now and then to correct her momentum. She went faster and faster, challenging the ground. Then she came to a street corner and had to stop for traffic.

Could I really make a magic spell? she thought. If I see a silver car pass before the light changes, my mother won't die. The light changed immediately, and she bit back a cry of dismay. I'm a child, she thought. A stupid child. No wonder they hardly ever let me see her for long.

There were only a few people outside school. It was still a long time until the bell. Zoë sat on the semicircle of stone wall that faced the flagpole to wait, but as she thought over the day's classes, she realized she had left her calculus textbook at home. She had thought everything she needed was in her locker, but now she remembered she had last seen it on top of the refrigerator. Perhaps she had time to go back and get it. No. If she left now, she wouldn't come back to school today.

That idea caught her fancy at once. Why should she go, anyhow? She couldn't possibly concentrate. How much could she get done? Lorraine does it all the time, she thought, and she doesn't get caught. And what if I did? I've got an excuse. A bitter snort escaped her lips. Yes, who would blame me? she decided. She got up at once and left the school grounds.

Zoë

Where did people go when they skipped school? Did the police really pick you up for truancy? She had cut a few classes before, but never the whole day. She walked back the way she had come but passed her home and went to the park.

It was too early for the young mothers and their pre-schoolers, but there were people anyway. Two scruffy teenage boys yanked on the swing chains and tossed the seats back and forth. Bandannas sprouted from the calves of their old blue jeans like weird, bedraggled plumage. Three swings were already wrapped all the way around the top pole. Vandalism comes to Oakwood, she thought with disgust. She hoped those rats hadn't been chewing away at the gazebo as well.

No use staying here. She didn't feel like answering a round of "Hey, baby" 's from some jerks in cutoff denim and leather. One of them looked like he'd been in a fight. Great, she thought. Another place I can't go. Just what I want, a bunch of heavy-metal maniacs invading my park.

But that was unfair. Simon wore leather, and he seemed all right. She remembered him standing in front of her, his nervous fingers unable to stay still, uncomfortable as she had been so many times. Then she had felt an empathy that had drawn her to him; now she saw what he'd been toying with. She drew her hand from her pocket and looked down. It was a star—like the one that lay in her palm, the one she had found on her back steps.

Anger and fear shook her. Nothing was sacred. Nothing

at all. She couldn't even go home. She felt violated. She had almost made him a friend. I want Mom, she thought.

The bus showed up, as if on command, as soon as she reached the bus stop. She couldn't turn back now. The rush-hour crowd had already thinned out, and there were plenty of seats.

At the hospital she swept by the reception desk without checking in. It's my right, she told herself. She's my mother. I belong here. She tried to look like she had business to attend to.

The elevator took forever to arrive, and when she got in, the car moved so slowly, she thought she'd scream. I suppose they don't want to give anyone a heart attack, she thought as she scuffed nervously at the brass plaque on the floor that said OTIS. When the elevator finally stopped, her heart gave a lurch—what if Mom was sick like last time? But she got off anyway.

She turned the corner by the nurses' station and kept on walking. Out of the corner of her eye Zoë saw the nurse there leap to her feet, but she wasn't going to stop for an interrogation now. She wasn't going to be put off. She had to talk to her mother. She knew the nurse was catching up by the rustle of petticoat against crisp uniform, so she ran the last few yards and flung the door open.

Her father looked up, startled, still clutching his wife's hand to his chest. The nurse arrived behind her. "What's going on?"

Zoë

"It's my daughter," Harry Sutcliff answered, almost as if he were reminding himself.

Our daughter, Zoë thought. She's not dead yet.

"I'm sorry," the nurse said, "but she looked so strange. It's okay?"

He nodded, so she left, leaving the door ajar.

"Zoë, what's wrong?" her father asked. He seemed to be grasping futilely for reasons for her to be there. Had the house exploded? Had there been an earthquake?

He was distracted by a raspy voice from the bed. "Why aren't you in school?" There was a quirky smile on her mother's face, half amusement, half something more bitter.

Her words gave him something to hold on to. "Why aren't you in school?" he repeated at Zoë, unaware of the inane echo.

"It's okay, Harry, really," her mother said in that whispery rasp. "What's a day here and there?" Tubes rattled softly as she tried to gesture gay abandon.

Zoë saw her father struggling not to argue. He had always been strict about stuff like that. "But how many days?" He stared at Zoë accusingly. "I haven't got room to worry about where you are every day, you know that, Zoë."

"First time, Dad. Honest."

"Well, you startled us." It was said begrudgingly. She didn't lie, he knew that. "You should think of your mother."

Zoë

"Harry," his wife gently chided.

"I do think of you, Mom," Zoë said. "All the time. I miss you, but the more I miss you, the less I'm allowed to see you."

She circled the bed to the opposite side from her father and took her mother's other hand. She had never seen a human being that color before, ashen blue. There seemed to be more tubes than ever, and her mother was lost amid the tangle. Oh, God. How can I tell her about that boy? she thought.

Her mother's eyes had not left her since she entered the room, but now they lowered, ashamed. "Sorry, Zoë," she whispered.

"Now look what you've done." Her father's brow was furrowed, as he fussed nervously with the bed sheets.

Zoë's mother gestured shakily for him to stop. "It's okay, Harry. You worry too much. I'm glad she's here. Really. Go and get me some juice. I want to talk to my daughter."

"You'll be all right?" he asked.

"Yes." She smiled, but it was tight and dry.

He left like a schoolboy on an errand, eager to please.

Zoë sat down.

"So tell me," her mother said, "what's going on in the outside world?" Her voice was weaker now that her husband had left, as if her strength were a show for his sake, to comfort him. Once again Zoë thought, I can't worry her with tales of teenage prowlers. But will Dad listen?

Zoë

"What's going on between you and your father?"

Zoë was startled into raising her eyebrows. "Nothing." No, that was dumb. On second thought, it was accurate.

"Nothing?"

"Really." Zoë slumped into the chair, chewing on her lip, wondering how much she could say.

"Out with it."

Zoë took a deep breath. "We never talk. He's never there. When he's home he's too tired to talk. It's like living with a robot. You're both here. I'm there. I'm lonely. There's no one to talk to." God, she sounded selfish—there's no one to talk to, whine, whine.

Her mother glanced away, fiddling nervously with a tissue. "Don't you ever talk about me?"

"He says that everything will be all right, or we'll talk about it later. Honestly, Mom"—it came out in a rush—"I don't feel like everything will be all right."

Her mother looked like she was about to say something, but changed her mind. She was silent for a while, her eyes closed, until Zoë thought she had fallen asleep.

"What about Lorraine?" she finally asked.

"Huh?"

"To talk to."

"Oh, Mom, you don't know." And it all tumbled out about Lorraine moving, of never seeing her, of missing her so much.

A nurse came in and interrupted to inject something into the flow from the IV bag, while Zoë looked nervously in

Zoë

the other direction. She couldn't speak until the nurse had left.

Her mother's eyes closed again, but she squeezed Zoë's hand once in a while to show she was listening. It felt so good. Once she said, "I'm so sorry, my love." And once, strangely out of sequence, "I'll speak to your father about it." Then she was truly asleep.

Zoë gazed at her, sorrow building in her throat. She looked tiny, and pale, and crumpled. Before this her mother's dying had been a possibility. People with cancer died. It was something Zoë worried about, had imagined a million times, but it had still seemed distant somehow. There had always been a vague hope. Now, looking at her mother so transparent and small, she knew for the first time that it was inevitable.

Her father came in and joined her in silent contemplation of the sleeping woman. She glanced at him. His eyes were tender. He held fruit juice in his hands as carefully as he would the water of life. Maybe I'm wrong, Zoë thought. Maybe she's stronger when he's around, because of the strength of his love.

"I'll walk you downstairs," he said, putting an arm around her. They went in silence, but she was used to that.

Down in the lobby he pointed to a pair of armchairs. "Let's sit for a few minutes." He closed his eyes and squeezed the bridge of his nose with thumb and forefinger; then he spoke. "I'm not going to preach to you about skipping school this time—goodness knows, things are rough for you right now—but I'm counting on you to carry on as usual, even if we aren't there to be in charge. It's one less thing to be worried about.''

Great, she thought. What about my worries? Doesn't he think I'm worried? Why doesn't he see I need to be here?

But he was still speaking. "And perhaps it's best if you let us know you're coming next time, okay?''

Anger swelled in her. Why was he locking her out? "No, it's not okay. It's like you want to keep her all to yourself and don't want to let me in at all. It's like you wish I never existed, so you wouldn't get your time with Mom interrupted. I wonder if you ever really wanted me at all.'' She felt sick saying it. It was unfair, and she knew it, but sometimes she really felt that way. And now it was said.

Her father looked at her with confusion. She'd never yelled at him like that before. She was ashamed at the hurt she saw on his face, and the spiteful power she couldn't help feeling.

"But, sweetheart,'' he said, "you've got it all wrong. How could you think that? We don't want you upset, that's all. Mom hates not seeing you, but you need to be with Lorraine more, taking your mind off things.''

Compassion tempered her anger, and she spoke carefully, as if to a child. "What do you think it's like waiting at home? Never knowing. Waiting for the phone to ring. This isn't the sort of thing you take your mind off easily. It's not like a test at school, or a visit to the dentist.'' Her hands were clutched beside her, knuckles white with the

73

grip as she tried to contain the fear she felt at speaking her mind. "Yes, it upsets me, but I've got to be part of this. I am part of this. Do you think she doesn't need me anymore?" She was dismayed to hear her voice tremble.

Her father sighed. "Yes, she needs you, she needs you all the time, but sometimes she can't bear you to see her this way. See her at the times she chooses—please, Zoë, for the sake of her dignity."

Zoë remembered her mother's embarrassed apology. It's Mom who doesn't want me here, she thought miserably.

"Don't either of you love me anymore?" she said.

There was a brief flicker of pain on her father's face.

"There's no profit in arguing," he said, trying to pat her shoulder.

Zoë wrenched her shoulder away. "You're right." She pushed herself from her chair and headed for the doors. She hadn't gotten anywhere. She still couldn't visit her mother when she wanted and, dammit, she hadn't even told them about the boy.

I made it worse, she told herself all the way home on the bus. I only wanted to ask what to do, and I made it worse. Poor Dad. He didn't even know that I was angry, until it burst out. They'll never let me back there now.

The house loomed cold and uncomforting, no longer safe. The rose by the front gate was withered and brown.

She thought about magic again as she lay on her bed and stared at the ceiling. If only there were some magic she could perform to stop her mother dying. If only she could put things right and make things how they used to be. "If only," she muttered to herself derisively, and sat up. "Who do you think you are? God?"

But the idea of magic had unlocked something. She pulled her notebook from her desk drawer and scribbled down lines furiously with a black felt-tip pen. She would worry about organizing later. Just let the words come. Then she went back and changed, deleted, and added. She forged the thoughts into form: the spells, the rites, the magic of life. Finally, she was satisfied. She had a poem— "Spells against Death."

Then she fell asleep on top the covers, her notebook clutched to her chest.

When she woke, she was surprised at how much time had gone by. It was after three already. Thinking she should eat something, she went downstairs.

After a nervous glance out the back-door window, she looked in the refrigerator. There was no milk, which meant she couldn't have cereal, so she settled on yogurt. She took it into the den and ate on the couch with her feet tucked under her, while she watched cartoons on television with the sound turned down.

Lorraine called just after three-thirty. "Why weren't you at school?"

Zoë didn't feel like explaining, it was too complicated. "I was sick."

Lorraine didn't even question it. "I can't come over this evening," she said. "I'm stuck packing and labeling. The

Zoë

movers are coming tomorrow. A couple of days on the floor in a sleeping bag, and we're off.''

Zoë didn't like the way Lorraine was starting to sound excited. "Is that all you can talk about?" It came out before she could help it.

There was silence on the other end of the line. Her cheeks stung with embarrassment. The embarrassment made her angrier. "I mean, all you talk about is yourself."

"Zoë, I phoned to find out how you were," came Lorraine's stricken words.

"Oh, I thought you phoned to tell me all about your great move."

"Well, I wouldn't have called if I knew you were going to be a bitch," Lorraine said. "I'll talk to you later, maybe." She hung up.

Zoë replaced the receiver with a trembling hand, the crash of Lorraine's phone still ringing in her ears. Why did I do that? What the hell was I doing? Hot tears scalded her face.

The house felt even emptier, looming and hollow. I'll go get milk, she decided. I need fresh air.

Walking didn't relieve the misery in her, however. I would like to do something drastic, she decided, and kicked a stone down the sidewalk in front of her. Something to make them notice me.

She picked up more cereal at the store, as well as milk, and some vacuum-cleaner bags. She was surprised, when she stepped outside, at how dark it had become above the streetlights.

Zoë

She was standing right by the alley where they had found that woman. She shuddered. Suddenly she remembered the boy standing at the same alley mouth, asking Lorraine to help him. Was that woman his mother? The thought appalled her. But, had they gone down the alley with him, could they have prevented it? Would the killer have heard them and run? Or was it already too late?

She turned into the alley, thinking "Spells against Death." It was too late for that woman, the boy's mother, but what about her mother? Was it too late for her?

The alley joined another that ran behind the stores, out to the street on either end of the row. A shortcut, she told herself. But it was darker than she thought inside. Lightning never strikes twice, she reassured herself as her jaw tensed, and she tightened her grip on the grocery bag.

Death had been here, but she would walk on through and show him what she thought of him, the cowardly thief. She held her head high, but her pace quickened.

The alley smelled of damp and garbage. A pile of boxes threw bizarre shadows in the light of a caged bulb by a back door. Was that where they'd found her? She tried not to look for dark stains on the ground.

What if there were someone back here? What if she were jumped? Would that be enough? Would death let her mother go? Only one Sutcliff needed, regardless of age or gender?

She was trying to make herself laugh at the thought, afraid to explore it, but a skittering behind a garbage can

Zoë

put an end to that. She turned the corner, her soft soles hitting cracked concrete silently. The alley beyond was dark, but there was light at the end, the warm glow of Elm Road. But something bigger than her moved in the shadows—in front, to the right, by basement stairs.

She edged to her left. What was it? Could she turn and run? Was it only a flickering of the dim light just past the steps? Yes, that's all. It made the shadows move unnaturally. She crept along, as close to the left-hand wall as possible.

A trash can got in her way. It went flying—empty, unanchored, smashing the silence, stopping her heart. The shadows leapt, too, from the steps into the light.

The boy crouched there shaking, eyes big as night. Blood smeared his face. Dripping feathers were clutched in his hand.

"Simon," she whispered.

Sorrow twisted his face.

She turned and ran.

· 8 ·

Simon

Simon hacked viciously at a broom handle with a large knife. He had stolen the knife that evening from the surplus store, shortly after he had made his decision. He muttered to himself fiercely as he worked, cross-legged, on the dusty classroom floor.

"She'll never let me in now. She'll never talk to me again." I need someone, a voice inside him howled. "Damn girl," he spat as the knife bit deep, then curled another slice of wood away from the pole.

What was she doing there anyway? What had possessed her to walk down that alley at that time? Stupid girl. Didn't she know better than to walk down dark alleys at night? Was she asking for trouble? "And I did want someone to talk to," he whispered, his eyes growing misty for a moment. But the moment passed quickly, and his eyes glittered again like hard, dark stones, as he carefully trimmed the last shreds of wood to leave a wicked point.

I have had enough, he thought, slapping the shank of the stick into his palm. I have waited too long. He stood and swatted at the dirt begriming his clothes. The dust of the grave seemed to follow him wherever he went.

"But never death," he muttered, "not for me, and never, ever love."

Like a shadow he could only live on the edge of people's lives, never touched or touching except to bring a cold shiver like a cloud over the sun, like a shroud over the corpse. The only time he touched, it was in death, yet that was the only thing that proved he existed at all.

"I know who's trapped me in this hell, and I know whose blood will wash the anger from my heart and help me sleep tomorrow."

Simon reached the shadow of the bushes in the Chestnut Street backyard, in time to see the boy climb out of his bedroom window onto the windowsill. The boy was dressed for climbing in a pair of overalls on top of a sweater. There were sneakers on his feet. So, Christopher roams tonight. A thin, glittering smile slid across Simon's face, and he stroked the sharp stick he held.

The boy edged along the windowsill and climbed down a drainpipe with the grace of a circus performer. There was a bundle across his back. When he reached the ground he untied something, sniffed the air as if testing it, and shifted the bundle to under his arm. Simon shrank farther into the shadows. As the boy crept past the shrubbery, Simon disincorporated slightly to blend in with the night. He would follow the boy to a more deserted spot, where a single cry would not set windows blazing with light.

Christopher walked with a purpose, once he reached the street. He kept to the inner edge of the sidewalk, away from the lights, but did not make as much effort to avoid attention as one would expect of a boy that size out late at night. The streets were mostly deserted, but outside one mock-Tudor cottage an elderly man stopped while unlatching the gate and stared at Christopher, ready to make comment. Simon, from across the street, could not see what kind of look Christopher gave the man, but it killed his question in his throat. He continued through his gate with a shrug of the shoulders.

Sometimes they slipped through dark backyards, both mere shimmers against the night. Too near houses, Simon thought, but I must reach him soon. The boy would sometimes stop and look around him puzzledly, as if seeking something. Shift, shift, Simon would urge his molecules, and drift into the night. But not too much, he warned himself, or I shall lose my thoughts as well.

He had lost himself like that once, for the devil knows how long. He had totally lost touch and drifted off until a rapidly changing air current had thrown him together again, and landed him naked in a roaring campfire. He had fled into the woods with the cries of alarmed hunters behind him, one screaming his Hail Marys at the top of his lungs.

Simon

Simon shuddered now at the memory of the awful burn on his leg that slowed his hunting for weeks. It would be worse, he thought as he crept from tree to tree, to be a semisapient cloud, never quite able to get back together again into corporeal form.

Christopher climbed a stone wall. Simon followed at a careful distance, scrambling up, hindered somewhat by the broom handle he held in one hand. Crouching at the top of the wall, he saw the boy turn from the street beyond and go left down Old Market Street toward the train station. With Christopher out of sight he did not slither down, but leapt in a joyful bound to the sidewalk and bounced his landing with animal grace, waving the sharpened broom handle above his head. The train station was lovely and quiet at this time of night. He hurried after so he would not lose his quarry.

Christopher stood at the entrance to the underpass, the dimly lit, tiled tunnel that led under the tracks to the ticket station in the middle, and across to the parking lot on the other side. The stairways that led to the tunnel were crooked and angular, and the light bulbs were often broken, leaving many dark corners. The entrance was well lit, however, and Christopher's bundle now assumed the shape of a teddy bear dangling from one of his small hands.

Simon settled into the rough stone of the embankment where the streetlights did not reach. Too light up here, he thought. Maybe he'll go down those steps. He licked his lips in anticipation.

Simon

But there was a click of heels in the distance. It came closer. A lone woman walked down the sidewalk, a smart red wool coat swaying with her determined step, a clutch purse tight in her hand. Maybe she was coming home after a date. Perhaps she had had an argument with her escort. Whatever, she was alone, and approaching the underpass. Simon stifled a groan. Not now.

She stopped when she saw Christopher. Simon heard the questioning tone of her voice, brisk yet kindly. Christopher chirped back at her, and she shook her finger at him, trying to be stern. He held a hand up to her, and she took it, unable to hide a smile. They turned and descended the underpass steps.

An oath burst from Simon. He struck out at the air with his pole and ran lightly for the tunnel mouth. He heard voices ahead, around the turn of the steps, and followed, shutting his senses against the damp, and the reek of old urine.

The woman's shoes clattered an echo in the chill air. Their voices ricocheted. The last train had come through an hour ago, so there was no thunder of wheels to challenge or drown them. Simon slunk silently behind. The station was closed for the night. The only ones possibly here would be the teenagers armed with spray paint, who declared their undying love all over the seeping walls, but no one ever saw them.

Simon turned to the left for the second flight down. The landing was dark; the light bulb smashed. Ahead he could see the woman and the child, down the tunnel, in a pool of light that seemed as if it could not quite break through the dirt. They were near the dark maw of the steps that led off to the right, to the platform. The mottled tunnel continued past it to the other side of the tracks, and another twisted stairway, that looked like a dead end. It felt as if it were raining above, when it hadn't rained for days. The floor was slimy in places. There were parts of the wall that looked cheesy, provoking the disquieting thought that if a person touched one of those places, his arm might sink in to the elbow.

All of a sudden the boy tripped and fell. He cried out in fear. The woman gasped, looked quickly around her in repulsion, but knelt on the filthy floor at his side anyway, laying down her purse beside his tumbled teddy bear. Simon stood in the shadows and watched the scene with a sneer on his face, his hands clutched tightly around the pole.

The boy was crying. He reached out to the woman, and she took him in her arms to comfort him. He burrowed himself into her coat, as if searching for warmth, while she patted him on the back. His head nestled in the hollow of her throat. His arms went around her neck—tightly.

Then she tried to pull back. Her eyes grew wide. She pulled at his arms, but they wouldn't release. She tugged at them harder. They were like a vise. She pushed at his head, but it wouldn't move. It was fast to the side of her neck. She started to scream. "You disgusting beast! You foul little animal!"

Simon

Her arms flailed wildly, her legs kicked, but she couldn't remove him. She tried to roll, but he had her pinned on her back with abnormal strength. He wound his hand in her hair to pull her head back more, and she tried to scream again, but it turned to a rattling gurgle as blood came out of her nose.

He moved his chin into her neck with a rhythmic push as if milking her. Her legs only twitched slightly now. Her arms lay useless at her sides. Her life flowed rapidly out of her veins into the small leech astride her.

Simon felt sick. He could almost hear the slurping and gulping of Christopher's gluttony. He couldn't take them gently. He couldn't take what he needed and leave the rest, leave some life. He had to take every drop they had and defile them in the process. He wasn't content with the blood, he wanted to feed on their fear. This woman had been let off easy, though. Simon had seen Christopher do much worse.

The woman's legs gave one last twitch, then lay still. An arm curved up, then fell to the ground with a meaty thud. Christopher dragged his head from her throat. He had his back to Simon.

Now, Simon thought, while he's sated with blood. He descended the stairs, his face grim. He raised the broom handle to waist level with both hands—a sharpened stake—and began a careful advance up the tunnel.

Christopher reached for something in the pocket of his dungarees. He pulled out a knife and quickly slit the woman's throat to disguise the fang marks. He wiped the knife on her coat, streaking a clashing smear into the wool blend. He stood up, still facing away, and pulled an arm across his mouth.

Simon drew closer, and closer still.

Christopher kicked the woman in the chest and grunted satisfaction.

Simon was almost there. He was too intent on his purpose to see the purse, and it skittered along the ground at his kick. Simon stopped, aghast. Christopher spun around to face him.

"Simon," he said, and was momentarily shocked, but he altered his tone to pleasant surprise. "How nice to see you again, dear. And so well prepared." He laughed, but it turned into a shrill giggle. His clothes began to writhe, bulge, and collapse. His face seemed to shrivel. The giggle changed to high-pitched squealing. All at once there was just a pile of clothes on the ground.

Simon dived for it, but a black shape struggled from the neck of the sweater and flapped to the ceiling. He threw the stake at it, but it flittered unharmed out of the tunnel, still squealing.

Simon cursed in every language he knew. He bent and picked up the pair of abandoned Oshkosh overalls, then flung them to the ground in frustration. The despicable boy could have transmuted his clothes too. One of their kind could shift the molecules of anything in close contact. He had left the clothes to taunt Simon.

Simon

Simon spat. He had better not linger with this corpse. He glanced over at the woman, shuddering at her grimace of death. There was something under her. Despite his repulsion he went over to explore.

It was the teddy bear, now spotted with blood. Simon picked it up. It was lumpy and hard, not a comfortable toy. There was a rip under one arm, and something pattered to the floor—soil. Simon smiled, then a chuckle rose to his lips. Soil.

Wham! Stars in his head. Blackness. He fell.

"I forgot something," a small, hard voice said, and the bear was snatched from Simon's hands.

"Thanks for the use of the stick," called the voice from far away.

His vision cleared before he had finished retching. The clothes were gone, but the stake lay at his feet where it had fallen after the blow. When the dry heaves abated, he pulled himself to his feet, using the slimy wall. He couldn't stay here.

It hurt his head terribly to move, but he did anyway. He had to find a place to hide. At least he had found out something important: if Christopher carried the soil with him, it was his last. He was afraid of losing it, and that was his weak spot. There would be many sleepless days if he lost it, and it would be a long journey to replace that native soil. He would become weaker and weaker along the way. Many things could happen in that time. If someone were to get hold of that soil . . .

Simon

But now that Christopher knew he was here, the wretch would be more alert. It would be harder than ever to trick him, almost impossible. Meanwhile, he'd start plans to move on. I've failed again, Simon thought. I'll never beat him. It was so unfair. With all he'd done, he'd never pay the price.

I'm so alone, he thought miserably. I'll be alone forever. There's no one to share my burden and make it lighter. He thought of Zoë, and the glimmer of life she kindled in him that he thought had been doused for good. It was useless. It could never be. The beast in him would not allow it, but he craved her nevertheless.

"If only." He sighed.

· 9 ·

Zoë

It wasn't until the first trick-or-treaters came that Zoë realized it was Halloween. When the doorbell rang, she had opened the door, puzzled, only to be confronted by a huddle of little goblins and witches. A smiling man waited for them by the front gate. All the children would be supervised this year.

"Wait a minute," she'd said, trying to cover her fluster, and raced to find her mother's stash of Three Musketeers bars.

The chocolate bars, and a bag of cookies she'd found in the back of a kitchen cabinet, had lasted through the first wave of tramps, monsters, and ghouls. Now she was down to the three jars of pennies her father kept on his dresser top. The pennies earned her some hostile looks. She was glad that the children were mostly young. If they hadn't been, she'd have been sure to gain a trick or two tonight.

Zoë

In between visitors she had changed into a long black evening gown of her mother's and combed her black hair carefully around her face. I hope the added atmosphere will take their minds off the lousy treats, she thought. It still needed something, however. She went to the hall closet and rummaged through her jacket pockets. She pulled out the small mottled box, opened it, and tied the crucifix Lorraine had given her around her neck with its red ribbon. Her reflection in the hall mirror pleased her, yet she touched a finger to the pendant sadly.

They hadn't spoken in two days. In fact, Zoë hadn't even seen Lorraine at school except for once in the hall yesterday, and Lorraine had turned on her heel and walked away. It was a relief, actually. She wouldn't have known what to say, how to explain.

I have to apologize, she told herself, just as she'd told herself over and over yesterday. But no matter how often she said it, she still couldn't seem to do anything.

"I'm such a jerk," she suddenly said out loud, and snatched up the phone.

The number jabbed automatically from her fingers, then she waited, almost holding her breath. The third ring was cut off short.

"Hello?"

"Diane." A reprieve, she thought. Time to ease into it. "Is Lorraine there?"

"Oh, I'm sorry, Zoë. She's spending the night at her mother's." She didn't sound sorry at all. "She won't be back till tomorrow morning."

Zoë

"Well, thanks, Diane, maybe I can call her there."

"I'm not sure that's a great idea, Zoë. It's their last night together for a while, you know. Monica probably wants Lorraine to herself tonight, not chattering forever on the phone. Be considerate, babe."

Like you care, Zoë thought. "Well, okay. Thanks."

"No problem. Bye." Diane hung up.

"Yeah, no problem," Zoë mumbled. Now, where was her phone book? She found it in the drawer and flicked through to find the number, but when she found it she started having second thoughts. Maybe Diane was right for once. Maybe she shouldn't call. I might not see her again, she thought. I can't let her leave on these terms. But Lorraine wouldn't be spending Halloween with her mother if I hadn't been such a turd, Zoë decided. She probably doesn't want to talk to me. She snapped the phone book shut.

She already missed Lorraine dreadfully. I don't want to be alone, she thought. She reopened the phone book tentatively and leafed through, looking for someone else to call. She realized that most of the girls she had listed were Lorraine's friends really, there was nobody she kept up with herself, and anyway, anyone in touch with reality would already have plans. As she leafed through the gilt-edged pages, she ran across Carol's number. Maybe she'd call her mother's friend. Carol is always kind, she thought, and I was pretty intense the last time I saw her. But the line was busy. She shut the book again and tossed it back into the drawer.

Zoë

Zoë was looking through her parents' records for some spooky organ music, when the next group came. Among them was a nasty little girl in a nurse's uniform, who poked her tongue out when she saw the pennies being tipped into her bag. She's lucky to get anything, Zoë thought. It's that or popcorn, and I know which one I would prefer. She found the record she was looking for after they left.

The doorbell rang again, and Zoë dispensed more pennies. The organ music seemed to be quite effective—eyes blinked, and bags were held out hesitantly. She hammed it up a bit with the witches' lines from *Macbeth*, as she dropped the pennies into the bags. Eye of newt was much more interesting than copper coins.

The second jar of pennies was now half empty, and the groups arrived farther and farther apart. Zoë was getting sick of the organ music, so she turned the stereo off.

The bell rang again, and she opened the door.

Simon.

She slammed the door shut. Her heart pounded in her chest.

He knocked this time.

"Go away."

"Please." She heard him faintly, muffled by the door. "Please let me in."

"Go away, or I'll call the police." She shot the dead bolt home, trembling.

"Why?" The voice was louder.

Zoë

"You know why." She leaned against the door, as if helping the locks to hold. Oh, God, I wish Lorraine was here, she thought.

"You would have told the police about me already, if you were going to."

"How do you know I didn't?" She hadn't, though. What could she tell them—she felt herself blush—that she had stupidly walked down a dark alley, at night, where there had been a murder, and seen a boy eating a bird? If she was crazy enough to go there, would they believe what she saw? "How do you know they're not waiting for me to let them know if you turn up?"

"Zoë, I've lived the darkest lie of all." His voice was sad. "I can recognize a lie."

Why did she believe him? "I can call them right now." She groped for a reason. "I'll say you're trying to break in."

"But I can't come in unless you invite me."

She heard a catch in his words, something like anguish. It didn't stop her from stepping toward the phone. His statement was absurd.

"It was just a bird, Zoë. You could see the feathers, surely?" It sounded as if he was kneeling by the mail slot now, because his voice was clearer.

She froze. He knew exactly what was bothering her, as if he had read her mind. She pictured again his beautiful face smeared with blood. Yes, she had remembered the feathers later. She had seen no body, no human body, only crushed feathers.

"I was hungry." He sounded miserable.

She shuddered. What kind of person ate raw birds? Could he be that desperate and hungry? Was he homeless and destitute enough to do that? Her disgust was almost tempered with pity. Or was he *really* sick, crazy sick? The pity fled, and she was shaking again. There had been a body later on that night, in another place. She had read about it in the newspaper the next day. Her mouth was unbearably dry.

"If you're sick enough to do that, you might do other things. You might be the killer they're looking for." There, it was out. Let him know she was on to him. She turned, hugged herself, and leaned with her back against the door.

"That's not me!" He sounded indignant.

"Maybe not"—though she wasn't sure about that—"but you're weird."

"I'll grant you that," he said quietly. There was silence just long enough to make her hope he'd left. She turned to the door again and cautiously bent down to the mail slot to look out.

"I know who the killer is."

She jerked upright, sucking her breath in sharply. Was it him? Was he playing games with her? "Then tell the police."

"They wouldn't believe me."

"Then why tell me?"

"I don't know yet. I thought you could help."

Zoë

"Help what, for Christ's sake? Bring him to justice?"

"I have to." His voice was hoarse with emotion. She was shocked by the intensity of his feelings. She slowly crouched on the other side of the mail slot, trying to make sense of the confusion she felt. A minute ago she thought he was a crazed killer; now she was wondering if he wasn't an aspiring, lunatic vigilante. God knows what was pushing him so hard. Was it delusion?

"Why do you care so much?" she asked, almost before she realized she was speaking out loud.

"He killed my mother." The voice broke.

My God, Zoë thought. I believe him. I don't want to, but I do.

"He's the cause of my loneliness."

Tears stung her eyes.

"But you've been spying on me." Dammit, she wasn't going to feel sorry for him; he was dangerous, crazy. "You were on my back steps. Why?"

He didn't even try to deny it. "Because you talked to me, and I felt like a person again. Maybe I hoped to catch a glimpse of you through the window. Maybe I hoped you would come out, and we could talk again. I don't know. Perhaps being close to you made me feel safe and real. Zoë, please let me in. I need you."

She could feel the truth of it in his voice. If she turned from him, would it be an act of cowardice, another hospital room she couldn't cross?

She stood up and pulled back the dead bolt. Oh, God,

she thought, I'm letting a crazy boy into the house, a crazy boy who eats birds. She slowly opened the door.

He was tall and slim. Beneath his tight black jeans and leather jacket she could sense lean, powerful muscles. Motionless, yet taut with energy, he was like a dancer a breath before movement. His dark clothing emphasized the pallor of his finely sculptured face and the ashy silver of his hair, fluffed to an almost airy, spiky texture. He reminded her of a thoroughbred animal gone feral. His eyes glittered to match the sparkling of the metal studs in the jacket he wore. She couldn't tell if it was just the light, or if he had tears in his eyes, like she did. But he winced as if the light from the house were too bright, and averted his face before she could tell for sure. That's when she noticed he was carrying something under his arm. It appeared to be a painting.

He held out a slender hand to her, but he made no move to enter. "You have to invite me in," he said. "I can't come in unless you ask." He waited for her answer with eyes lowered.

There was probably a name for this type of behavior in psychology textbooks, she decided. "Come in, Simon."

A smile lit his face, although he seemed too shy to look at her.

That face could break a heart, she thought. It was suddenly hard to think of him as a murderer.

"You had better sit down," she said, and wondered where to take him. She led him to the den, and he gazed around as he followed her. "Would you like something to drink?" She was unsure of this new role as hostess.

He glanced at her, then smiled faintly. "I've been fed at the breast of death, and no other food now can sustain me."

She giggled nervously. "Is that yes or no?" Good grief, listen to me, she thought. How sophisticated.

"Sorry," he said stiffly. "It's something I wrote once. I never thought I'd see the day when an opportunity arose to use it. I couldn't resist."

He writes? Her eyebrows went up a little.

"I am not illiterate," he said, piqued at catching her surprise, in another of his swift glances. "And I don't want any of your beverages."

"Well, I think I'll have something." She left to get a Coke. He's as jittery as I am, she thought. She took her time in the kitchen, time to steady her nerves and take a few deep breaths.

When she came back, he was fiddling with the radio. The painting he had carried in was propped up on the couch. He found a rock station that seemed to suit him and came over to stand next to her in front of the gilt-framed portrait. He still wouldn't look at her, and it was beginning to bother her.

He reached out as if to put an arm around her shoulders, and she stepped aside hastily. "No," he said, sounding anxious to reassure her. "I just want your necklace."

She wondered why, so she stood still as his fingers

97

nimbly untied the knot and freed the crucifix from around her neck. He dangled it gingerly by its ribbon at arm's length and, for the first time since he had entered, looked her full in the face. Without taking his eyes from her, he deposited the crucifix in a ceramic jar on the coffee table, with uncanny accuracy. "The dress is beautiful, but that thing doesn't suit you."

She was angry but afraid to protest. Let it lie, she thought. It's not important enough to fight over. And she moved away to sit in an easy chair with the coffee table between them.

To her relief he didn't follow, but sat on the couch and looked around the room. He relaxed into the cushions like a cat at home, all nervousness now gone. He seemed especially interested in the paintings on the walls. He rubbed his hands as if warming them by a fire. "I have a painting too," he said unnecessarily.

The Ramones filled the air around them with pulsing music. "I love rock," he said. "I have ever since it started. There's something elemental about it. It's the pounding of blood through veins. Before that there was the blues, and jazz—I liked that, too, but not this way. Not this heart-thumping way. They didn't allow music in the village I was born in, you know, but I've had plenty of time to make it up since."

"Psychotherapy. Psychotherapy," the lyrics pounded.

He turned dreamily to face the painting he had set up on the couch. "I wanted you to see this."

Zoë

Slow motion, Zoë thought.

"Come look." He beckoned her.

Curiosity lured her, and she knelt on the floor in front of the couch, pushing the small glass-topped table askew with her feet. The frame was battered and chipped, and one corner had been crushed. The painting within looked old. It was a family portrait: a stern man in black, with a large white collar, stood by a chair where a woman, also in black, sat with a baby in her lap. A small boy of about six stood proudly in front of his father, dressed in the same severe clothes. He reminded her of someone. The painting was full of shadows. The furniture was sensible, and their expressions somber. Well, perhaps not the woman's. It seemed like she was trying very hard not to smile; her eyes sparkled, as if she were too merry to stay solemn for long.

Zoë looked up questioningly at Simon.

"My family," he said.

"You mean your ancestors?"

"My parents and brother."

Zoë frowned. She wasn't sure if she really felt like dealing with this. "Like those fake old photos you can have taken?" she asked. "Dressed up like cowboys or something?"

Simon turned the painting around and handed it to her. There was faded brown writing on the back, a date— 1651—and words that curled in unexpected ways. *Edmund Bristol Gentleman and his ladie wyfe* (she couldn't read this part) *their sons* (unintelligible again).

Zoë

"It was the year Old Rowley came back behind a Scottish army," Simon said. She stared at him. "He became Charles II," he explained, "but not that year. Cromwell sent him running at Worcester."

Zoë waved him quiet, impatiently. "What does that prove? People can fake that stuff."

He took back the painting firmly and turned it around again. He looked at it longingly. "That's me," he said, pointing at the baby.

Oh, no, she thought.

"And that's your killer," he said, pointing at the other child. "My brother, Christopher."

"How can you expect me to believe that?" she cried, and started to stand up. He grabbed her hand in an icy grip and held her there while he awkwardly slid the painting between the end table and the couch. This was a mistake, she thought, a stupid mistake.

"He waits by dark places," Simon continued.

Oh, no, it's not you. Please, it's not you, Zoë begged silently.

"He tells women he's lost, then he takes advantage of their kind hearts." Simon's eyes burned, terrifying her. "He leads them into the dark and slaughters them, then cuts their throats." His grip tightened with the urgency of his words. "He looks like a child, but he's old as sin, and he's bloated with filth and corruption. They think he's only a child."

Zoë grew colder and colder, as if the chill of his hand

were seeping into her. She saw back to the little boy at the
alley's mouth, talking to Lorraine. "I'm lost," he had told
her. She trembled. He's tricking me somehow, she thought.
But no, she'd never told him about that. How could he
know? My God, she realized. It could have been Lorraine
lying there dead. No, it wasn't true.

"He killed my mother," Simon was saying. "She was
overjoyed to have him again, but he killed his own mother
in the filthiest way. And he knew who she was. I have
followed him for a long time, and now I have found him.
But I failed, Zoë. I tried to kill him, and I failed. What am
I to do?"

Let me go, she wanted to scream.

His grip softened. His hand moved up her arm. She
tried to move back but found herself leaning forward
instead. She saw a crackling of summer lightning in his
eyes—the heat lightning she had felt the night he walked
her home. He needed her. After weeks of not feeling
needed by others, it seemed welcome. His lips touched
hers, cool, soft, almost chaste. I can't believe I'm doing
this, she thought. He moaned slightly, as if it were his first
kiss, long denied, and she gently folded into him while he
put his arms around her. Her mouth parted. He nibbled her
lip.

"Ouch!" She pushed him away.

His eyes were large, dark, and compelling. He blinked,
and suddenly she felt like she was waking from a dream.
He looked ashamed. "I'm sorry," he said. "I made you

Zoë

kiss me. I wasn't going to. I wanted you to come to me of your own free will. But the chance was slipping away. I was afraid I was losing any chance with you."

"That's absurd," she said indignantly. "You didn't make me kiss you." Her heart beat fast, and her lip tingled where he had bitten her. "What makes you think you could do that?"

"I am not like you," he said. "I am not human anymore, I think."

She frowned. She didn't want to be reminded of his strangeness; she wanted to be held, and to forget it. She had never enjoyed a kiss like that before. She climbed up beside him on the couch, but embarrassed by her desire to be kissed, she found she couldn't look at him directly. She absently brushed her mouth, and it left a smear of blood on her hand. He leaned to her and gently licked her lip. She felt like she was melting, but he shivered as if he were cold. She pulled back, afraid of her response.

"I will tell you a story," he said, with a slight tremble to his voice, "and then you will believe me."

· 10 ·

Simon

$\mathfrak{S}$imon turned off the radio. No distractions now, he thought, no matter how much I like the music. Motorhead was abruptly silenced. He settled back on the couch next to Zoë and began his tale.

"I was born in a village outside Bristol—that's in the west of England. My father owned a fair amount of land, upon which he raised sheep, and he sold cloth locally. But he was ambitious." Simon saw Zoë sink into the cushions, relaxing into the tale.

"In those days Parliament ruled. The old king was dead, and the king-to-be still in exile. They were grim times, when the slightest hint of pleasure was condemned as sin. The maypole was cut down, and Christmas was forbidden except as a fast. This made life difficult for my mother, because she had a happy nature, and was fond of dance and song, but was forced to wear dark colors and keep a solemn look on her face in public. Yet in her own home she sang to her children at night, and the neighbors be damned. She had a merry laugh, and all who knew her said it was hard not to join her in a prank.'' Simon reached over the arm of the couch and stroked the picture frame gently as he talked. It was all he had left of her.

''My father's business was just starting to do well when I was an infant, so he commissioned this portrait to record his good fortune. It was shortly after this portrait was painted that Wulfram von Grab came into our lives.'' Simon's spine stiffened. He saw Zoë look at him curiously, and tried to relax.

''My father would always say that, whatever else the faults of puritan rule, the Lord Protector had opened up more chance of trade in Europe than any of the Stuart kings. Businessmen with political good sense were offered a golden opportunity to succeed, and my father took more and more trips to the city. On one of those trips he met von Grab. Von Grab said he could help my father take advantage of the thriving market for British broadcloth on the Continent, in return for a percentage, of course. Since he had contacts my father could benefit from, my father brought him home to discuss it further.''

Simon saw the question on Zoë's face before she voiced it. How would he know all this? ''Of course, I only heard of this when I was older, and in dribs and drabs, but I gathered enough to put the story together.

Simon

"Von Grab was a tall, pale man, with a mane of dark hair—rumored to be a frivolous wig—and darker eyes. He moved gracefully and punctuated his animated conversation with quick gestures of his long, elegant hands. He made himself a pleasant guest and won my mother over quickly with jokes and songs. He was, in turn, quite taken with my brother, Christopher.

"No matter how charming my parents found von Grab, the servants thought him odd. Whether this was because he was European, or because he was truly eccentric, they couldn't say, but at a time when people rose at dawn, he slept past noon, and while the family went to bed not much after dusk, they knew that he was awake well into the night. He hardly ate at all, claiming a weak digestion, although he liked a good red wine; and he never attended chapel. But he had plenty of money, and was likely to make my father rich, so his strangeness was overlooked.

"Von Grab rarely ventured outside, but he did enjoy sitting by the fire after supper, spinning a tale or two, and even the few servants would creep into the shadowed drawing-room to hear his fanciful stories.

"They say Christopher was spellbound. He would sit at the visitor's feet, or on his knee, and beg for one more tale. While Mother looked on amused, von Grab would laugh and tousle Christopher's light brown hair—the hair that is now white—and call him his sweet angel, his little

Fledermaus. Christopher spent as much time as possible with him. My mother judged von Grab to be an affectionate man and chided him gently for not having a wife."

Zoë shifted restlessly, and Simon motioned for her to be still. "I'm getting to the point.

"One night my father's manservant was slipping secretly through the hall to visit the scullery maid, when he heard soft voices on the upstairs landing. Creeping partway up the stairs, he saw von Grab at his door, talking to Christopher, who stood there in his nightshirt, looking small and hollow-eyed in the candlelight. The servant assumed the boy had had a nightmare and gone for reassurance to his friend, so he withdrew. He was not eager for anyone to know he was up and about at this hour.

"Perhaps von Grab knew he had been seen and thought the seeds of suspicion had been sown, or perhaps he couldn't wait any longer. I can only imagine. But the next night he left after all were sleeping, taking only a few belongings on his black mare, and nobody knew until the morning after, when the whole household was searching for Christopher.

"That morning the child's bed had been discovered empty by the housemaid, and he couldn't be found anywhere. Finally, when my mother was thoroughly panicked and the house was in an uproar, my father's manservant had to put aside his embarrassment and tell what he had seen. My father knocked on von Grab's door, but no one responded, and the door opened easily onto an empty room. The bed had not been slept in. Wulfram von Grab had gone, and Christopher with him.''

Zoë leaned toward Simon. Her expression was serious and intent. He had her within his tale now.

"My father wrote letters frantically to the men von Grab had always mentioned as his associates, and sent them off by servant to the nearest posthouse. Messengers were dispatched to the ports. Then he left for Bristol, to visit the inn where he had met von Grab. But no one had seen the foreigner, and a search of Bristol proved useless. My father had to come back, lackluster, to his business, and trust in God and his letters.

"One by one his messengers returned with nothing to report, and when the replies to his letters came back, they plunged him into despair. None of those men even knew who von Grab was. 'How can this be?' my father asked all around him. He was too godly and innocent to see harm in a man's attentions to a young boy. He could never have conceived of what came later.

"With nothing more to do, gradually the household fell back into its normal routine. But really, it would never be the same. My father announced that we should put the tragedy behind us, and flung himself mindlessly into his work. His business flourished, and even one of von Grab's supposed contacts offered to sponsor my father's ventures on the Continent, when he heard the painful tale. My father grew richer, but always, anyone who traveled for him had strict orders—to look for Christopher.

"My mother never ceased mourning. Her smiles were fewer, and she became nervous, jumping if even a branch scraped a window." Simon tried hard to visualize the mother who had loved him so long ago, but he couldn't see her face anymore, except by looking at the picture, although he remembered her softness and warmth. He sighed. "And she loved me with a desperate fierceness that even a small child found binding at times. She had not protected her firstborn, so she seldom let me out of her sight. Perhaps God was punishing her; she didn't know. When the villagers whispered it must be our family's sin that had led to this tragedy, she stopped going to chapel on Sundays. She would punish God.

"Then, when I was four years old, she started seeing Christopher—peering in the window at night, hiding in the shadows of a darkened room, or standing outside in the moonlight. 'There he is,' she'd cry. At first my father would jump to look, or a servant would rush outdoors, but there was never anyone there. Soon they just shook their heads. My father would stroke her hair sadly and try to comfort her, but she would get more and more hysterical as people refused to believe her.

"One of my few, and most vivid, memories of my mother is of her sitting me in my father's wooden chair one night. 'Be a good boy,' I can still hear her say. 'Stay right there. I will not be long.' She was smiling, I think. I remember because it was so unusual. She opened a window and called to someone outside; then she left the room, left me in the cold night breeze coming through the casement. I never saw her again." Simon realized he was holding himself against that remembered cold. But that cold is always with me now, he thought.

"They found her later, in the garden, with her throat slashed."

Zoë drew in her breath sharply and held her hand to her own throat. The movement caught Simon's eye. He reached over and lowered her hand. Her eyes were large, and he found compassion there. How strange, and wonderful, and sad to tell this story to someone after so long a time, and have her care, he thought. He wanted to touch her face, but he kept his hands to himself. He wouldn't distract from his tale.

"I was cuddled and cosseted by all, and didn't understand the tears, but I had enough of my own for many nights after, when my mother never answered my calls. She was a sweet and gentle woman with a happy spirit; she'd never deserved her lot in life.

"Soon after that my father moved our household to the city of Bristol. He couldn't bear to live in that house any longer. He made a good profit from the land he sold and added several imports to his business. I was under the care of servants mostly—we had more now—and I hardly ever saw my father. I remember being angry at him for not making my mama stay, but maybe I was more frightened that he himself wouldn't come back. Who's to say? But we were never close after that time.

"We didn't stay in Bristol for long. In my eighth year, the same year Cromwell died, my father decided it would be better for his business if we moved to London. We were settling into our new house on Eweskin Lane at the same time that the new king was settling back into Whitehall.

"As I grew up, wrestling with the classics under the rule of a strict tutor, London was changing drastically from the city it had been under the Commonwealth. A springtime came to the city, and the people shed their blacks and whites and bloomed with bright colors. When plague and the Great Fire left us unscathed, my father decided that perhaps now God would allow us some measure of peace.

"But as I became a young man, I wasn't much to my father's liking. The clothes he wore were still understated grays and browns, although of the finest cloth. I, however, fell in tune with the times and spent my ample allowance on the bright silks and laces that were again the fashion. I was always ready to buy a garter to set off my shapely calf." Zoë smiled. "But I ignored my father's pleas to continue my studies, or even to join him in the business. 'You have made the money,' I would say, 'what need you of me?'

"I took to parading at Covent Garden and the Royal Exchange with the gallants and fops, and hoped to become friends with some titled gentleman. I expect they called me

Simon

an upstart tradesman's son behind my back, but I was witty and had the money to buy them drink, so I was hailed heartily whenever I showed up.

"There was a tavern where my friends liked to while away the evening. It was called the Boar and Charter, but for a joke we called it the Whore and Garter, because there were willing young ladies there who would share our supper, and more. I would dawdle there long past decent hours and would come home late, often the worse for drink. This upset my father, and we had many fights over it, which only encouraged me to stay away more. But he never had the heart to take away my funds, although he threatened to disinherit me more than once. I was spoiled and didn't know it. It seemed to me that he always had more time for his business than for me. I suppose it was his way of blocking out his pain, but I thought he didn't love me. If my mother had been alive, it would have been different.

"In those days there were few lamps lit on the street, and it wasn't safe to walk alone at night; but for a few pennies you could hire a linkboy to light you home. Some of them loitered outside the tavern, waiting for customers. I often used them. There was one, though, a pale waif, younger than the rest and new to the trade, who had a habit of staring at me. I had no idea why, but it made me shudder, and I avoided him."

Simon stopped for a moment, wrinkling his brow. He wanted to remember everything. It had happened so long ago, sometimes it seemed more like a dream. Zoë sipped her drink that had sat untouched for a while. "Go on," she said. He picked up a small ashtray from the table and shifted it from hand to hand as he searched for the words.

"One night, when I left the tavern, drunk as usual, there was a scuffle at the corner. Two linkboys were fighting. The larger one yelped and ran off, and the small, pale boy approached me with a lamp. 'Want a light, yer lordship?' I laughed at his nerve, too drunk to be particular, and waved him on in front of me, mumbling my destination. I stumbled along after him and had to stop more than once to piss against a wall. Once I fell heavily into a post at the street edge and swore like a Wapping waterman, a skill I was proud of.

"There was a fog rolling in, but I was too numb to feel the chill. 'You're awful young for this game, nipper,' I called. 'I'm older than I look, yer lordship,' he said. Soon the fog was so thick that the boy's lamp barely fought back the darkness. A sudden squall of rain spattered me, and I must have groaned, for the boy turned to look at me. 'Feelin' all right, sir?' he asked, and suddenly I wasn't."

Simon smacked the ashtray down on the tabletop. Zoë flinched and moved the ashtray away from him. "Sorry," he muttered. "But I know it wasn't just the drink that made me sick. He was doing something to me. My stomach felt queer and my head hot. The boy's eyes were swirling orbs that seemed to bulge hugely while his body receded. I tore my gaze from him and looked about me. I wasn't sure where we were.

" 'You're ill, sir,' he said, taking my hand in his cold little fist. 'There's a gentleman I know lives near here. He'll take 'ee in.' He began to lead me, and I followed, wishing more than anything to lie down.

" 'Where are we?' I asked, but then we were at a door, and the waif was knocking. He stared at me intently while we waited for an answer, and I began to sway. I remember vaguely the door opening, the boy whispering to a nightcapped maid, then burly arms around me. Someone must have put me to bed, for all I remember then is the nightmare.

"I was spinning. There was something buzzing around my head—a giant fly. I kept on hitting at it, but it wouldn't go away. It kept on brushing at my face with black whiskers, biting at me, and it smelled like carrion.

"I woke several times to find myself in a bedchamber, with a terrible itching about my neck and shoulders, but I felt so weak, I could never keep my eyes open. One time there was a man beside my bed. He was dark and handsome, like our king, with a black mustache and a long curling wig, yet he had the palest face. I was a little more aware this time and tried to talk, but all that came out was a croak.

" 'Calm, calm,' he said in a voice strangely soothing,

despite its guttural tone. He stroked my head with long fingers. 'You have a fever.' He made a motion, and the linkboy came into my line of vision. 'My imp here will feed you broth for your strength.'

"I was confused. Was the child a street boy, or this man's servant? But my eagerness for the broth wiped away my questions, and I slobbered like an infant. The soup loosened my throat. 'My father?' I was finally able to ask.

" 'We have sent a message,' the man said. 'You gave the boy your address, remember? He will come when he can.' I didn't remember, but neither did I think my father would rush to be by my side. They must have seen the look of derision on my face. 'A man's business can't always wait,' the man said, and left the room as if taking his own advice.

"I noticed blood on the sheet. 'You were scratching yourself in your delirium,' the boy said, following my eyes. 'I almost bound your hands.'

"I would have asked for my clothes, but I was suddenly overcome with drowsiness again, and fell into another fitful sleep.

"I don't know how long I was there, but it must have been days. The dreams plagued me, but the boy was always there when I woke. One time I saw the man come in and curse, as if taken by surprise. He cuffed the boy and sent broth splattering across the room. Before I lost consciousness, I heard him say, 'No more soup.' But I took that for a dream also, because the boy came often to feed me, and when he did I felt stronger.'' Simon took Zoë's hands, and held them as if belief were something he could send her through his fingertips.

"Then, one night, I briefly broke through the dreams." His grip tightened as he talked. "And I found myself clutched to the breast of my elegant host." He couldn't look at her now, while he told her this. He didn't want to see the disgust he felt echoed on her face. "There was sharp pain at my throat where his head lay. I started to struggle and to make noise, even then misinterpreting his actions, my young manhood offended. He pulled away and hit me. He looked furious. It wasn't the look of a sane man. His face was flushed, his eyes were red, and blood smeared his mouth. Then he saw the fear in me, and his lips drew back in a delighted snarl—they revealed dripping yellowed fangs."

Zoë pulled her hands from Simon with a squeak of protest and rubbed her fingers. Simon glanced in surprise at his own hands, yet continued speaking.

" 'Perhaps I was too enthusiastic tonight,' the man said, his anger turning to amusement. 'There are a few nights left in you yet, I should not ruin them.' He left me screaming hoarsely but too weak to move. I must have fainted.

"I awoke to find the boy there beside me. I cringed away. 'The soup will return your strength for only so long,' he said matter-of-factly, 'and that time has passed. If you wish to escape my master, then further actions are necessary.'

" 'What?' I whispered, hope rising. But then I was suspicious. 'Why?'

" 'Because he beats me. Because he holds from me what I desire. Because I hate him. Is that enough? I am tired of doing his dirty work and luring prey like you to his den, because he's so disgustingly old and jaded, it bores him to do it himself.'

"It would save my life, so I nodded acceptance, and the boy told me his plan. 'He cannot feast upon his own. If I make you like him, he cannot kill you.'

"I did not think it possible to be sicker than I already was, but my stomach heaved." Simon grimaced, feeling sick at the memory. "I struggled to rise. 'No!' I tried to cry, but it came out as a frightened squeak.

" 'Do you want to die?' he whispered fiercely. 'It's your only choice.' I couldn't speak. 'It's not so bad,' he said. 'You don't have to be a beast like him. He made me, and I'm not awful, am I?' I moved as far away from him as I could on that tiny bed. He reached for me anxiously. 'You don't have to prey on humans; animals suffice. You eat animals anyway.' I tried to shake free of him, but he held tighter. 'It's your only chance,' he insisted. He stroked my clammy brow and smiled. 'I could change you anyway, against your will, but I wouldn't want to do that. I wouldn't want to force you. I want to save your life.' He repeatedly stroked my brow, lulling me, and I relaxed and foolishly took comfort in it. 'I want to save your life,' he repeated. 'He'll kill you!'

"And, Zoë, I was so frightened, so weak, and so afraid of dying, I ignored the screaming inside of me, and believed his lies. Heaven help me, I said yes."

Simon felt her warm hand on his and realized he had not been seeing this room at all. His eyes focused on Zoë, and he felt ashamed at the compassion on her face. It was a second before he could speak again.

"He opened my shirt. I didn't know what to expect. Quickly, he sliced my chest with a clawlike nail. I whimpered—then I saw his fangs and gave up hope. He was torturing me. He was like the other. But he swiftly snicked his own wrist and held it to my chest. Our blood mingled there as I stared down in disbelief. 'To make sure,' he said, and held out his wrist to me. I looked at him uncomprehendingly. 'Suck,' he said, and I jerked my head away. But he grasped my hair with a grip beyond the strength of a child and forced my head around. 'For your life,' he hissed. And choking back the bile, I drank his blood, while he lapped mine up directly above my heart. I sucked till he pulled his wrist away.

"That is the way our kind are born, Zoë. It takes the sharing of blood. Our victims, when they're drained, well—they're just dead. They don't rise again. Not unless, in

117

their final weakness, they share the blood of one of the damned.

"While I watched in horror, the boy held his arm out for me to see as the blood dried and flaked off, the skin curled back together with a will of its own, the cut on his wrist sealed, and the scar faded away into nothing. 'No one can hurt you now,' he said.

"And it's true, Zoë. No matter what has happened to me, the only scar I have is the one he gave me."

"Show me," Zoë said, challenging him.

Simon smiled sadly. He slipped the jacket off in a creaking of leather and pulled the T-shirt over his head, tousling his hair. Zoë ran a burning finger along the scar, from above his left nipple in a streak to his right ribs. He closed his eyes. Her touch seared his marble-cold flesh deliciously, and his nipples hardened; he was aware of the cold even more because of her. He pulled her to him. Take away my cold, he thought. Make me warm again. She trembled, and he thought perhaps it was not from fear, but because she had never been held to a man's naked chest before. Yet she wrapped her arms around him. How long, he thought, since a beautiful girl trembled for me alone, and not because of my power to hypnotize. He continued his story, holding her tight against the cold.

"I crashed into a dark and dreamless sleep; the sort of sleep where a person loses contact with his very existence. I think that was when I died.

"When I woke up again, I had changed. I felt as if a

118

cold sun were glowing within me and growing larger. With it came power. All through that day anger built in me, as my strength grew. The animal side of me was rising. Finally, I lay there rigid, staring at the ceiling, awaiting my tormentor, not knowing yet what I would do, and terrified by my rage.

"The door finally squeaked open, and I feigned sleep, not knowing what else to do. The man came to me where I lay, and I heard his breath rasping greedily as he bent to me. His weight on the bed rolled me against him. When he put his loathed face to my neck, I was mindlessly ready to strangle him, but his fangs sank into my vein, paralyzing me for that moment. But then he wrenched back. He spat. He snarled. He pushed himself off the bed with a force that shattered the frame, and threw me against the wall. 'Boy!' he screamed, whirling to face the door. 'Boy! What have you done?'

"I pulled myself across the broken bed toward him as the boy came hurtling through the door with a look of glee on his face. 'Despicable puppy,' my captor said. 'You dare defy me?' He lurched for the boy, and the beast broke through in me." Simon saw that other room again and felt that surge of hate. "I looked around madly for a weapon and snatched what was at hand. Stumbling from the bed, I flung myself at him. I ran him through with a shard from the ruined bedpost." Simon felt Zoë shudder as she made a sound of disgust. "He fell to the floor, jerking and twitching. His dark wig slid from his head, revealing frosty hair. His skin fell in. He shrank. He writhed. Finally he lay still, a shriveled monkey of a thing, scarcely human.

"The boy kicked the corpse and grinned. 'How clever,' he said. 'Much better than what I had in mind.' I was shaking so badly, I could hardly spare much amazement for his words." Simon paused, aware of how tightly Zoë held him. 'I'm rich now,' the boy said. 'The fool willed me all his goods, never expecting me to inherit, of course. The servants will get rid of this—I have already promised them much for their loyalty. We will have a fine time together, Simon.'

"This was the first time he had used my name. I did not remember telling it. 'Why together?' I asked. 'Why me?' And he answered, 'When you look like a child, you need a protector, someone who stands as a guardian in others' eyes. Who better than one's own brother?' "

Zoë released Simon and sat back. "Christopher," she said.

He nodded.

"I thought so." Yet she looked shocked.

"Yes, it all fell into place—who the man was, who this child, if I could profane the word, was." Simon turned from Zoë. He would hate even more telling the next part. He placed his hands lightly on the coffee table and continued, head bowed, feeling the ice rise again within him.

Simon

" 'You will get stronger,' Christopher told me, 'but the color will fade from you as your blood changes. Your heart will cease to beat, yet, nevertheless, your blood will crawl through your veins. You will take in air out of habit only; you will need it to speak but not to live. And you will shun the day and its burning rays, because the daylight is for the living and the sun rejects us. You will live by night. But what power you will have! The power to suck the very essence of life itself and bend others to your will. You will live a long, long time—time enough to accumulate wealth and to afford many pleasures. We will be good together, Simon. You won't be like Mother.'

" 'What do you mean?' I demanded, dreading the answer.

"And Christopher told me. 'Wulfram wanted me to kill her to prove I was loyal to him. I didn't like it much and offered her a chance. But she turned from me. She didn't love me anymore.'

" 'Mother?' I said, softly at first, in shock. 'You killed Mother?' I asked louder. Then, 'Mother!' I screamed."

Zoë shrieked and jerked back. The table had cracked. The glass was rimed with frost. Simon shook.

"I hurled myself at him, but I was slammed to the ground. I didn't expect it from one his size. He grinned at me and gloated. 'As I said, you will grow stronger—but not now. I am the strong one now.' He turned.

" 'Oh, who do you desire for your first meal?' he asked casually over his shoulder as he left. 'Shall I bring home your favorite girl from that tavern of yours?'

Simon

"I pulled myself from the floor. 'You said *animals*.'

" 'I lied,' he said through the crack of the door. It closed, and I heard him slide a bolt home outside. It was then I realized what I had done.

"I stumbled frantically around that room looking for another way out, but there was no other door. I wrenched down drapery, meaning to flee through a window, but found none, just blank wall. I pummeled the locked door with useless fists and battered my shoulder against it, to no avail. I even tried to dig through the wall with a spoon, but the room had to be underground, with rock behind the plaster, for all the impression I made. I gave up, exhausted, and flung myself back on the shattered bed. I was trapped, and damned, with only a hideous corpse for company. Maybe that was when I started to go mad."

Simon suddenly noticed the table and removed his hands. There were no cuts.

"He brought me a girl that night, a cringing young thing. I refused to go near her. 'You will.' He laughed and dragged her away.

"Yet night after night I refused, and he grew angrier each time. But I was growing weaker, and every time he brought me the offering it was harder to resist. Finally, he brought her in bound, and slashed her throat with a kitchen knife so the blood would run freely. He took his fill in front of me until his ploy worked, and the smell of fresh blood drove me wild. I made a mess of it while Christopher laughed and laughed, as if it were a great joke. But the joke was on him, for he'd given me the power to overcome him. To his surprise I knocked him aside and ran from that room, from that detested house, out into the streets.

"I ran and ran.

"I remember retching in an alley, wiping my mouth over and over with the only thing I wore, a ragged, blood-soaked shirt. But after that my mind broke with the guilt and disgust.

"I must have found my way to the outskirts of the city, to the fields, then to the woods. I don't know how I survived. Don't ask me what I did, because I have few memories of that time. I became a mindless animal. I did find that Christopher was right after all. You can survive on animals for a time, but it never satisfies—the hunger is never totally sated, it never leaves you, and it hurts. I know I killed people when I could find them, and anything else when I could not.

"It was years until my senses began to come back, and I made my way into the world of men again. By that time I was used to the killing, but never to the disgust afterward. As my memory returned, I swore to avenge myself on Christopher, for my mother's sake—for mine.

"I have followed him for many years."

"How did you trace him after all that time?" Zoë asked.

Simon smiled sadly. "It was easy, really. I followed

reports of a certain type of violence—girls disappearing or found mutilated. Three times I even came face-to-face with him. I almost had him in London in the eighteen eighties, but he got away.''

"How did you get here?''

"I came over in the thirties. An ocean-liner murder reported in the paper tipped me off. I was terribly sick all the way.''

Zoë shook her head, "No, I mean this town.''

"Oh. . . . There was a mysterious spate of deaths at an orphanage. I had lost Christopher's trail a year before. He had left such a disquietingly obvious trail of child pornography, it was as if he were taunting me, but suddenly there was no more evidence; the trail dead-ended just when I was getting close. The orphanage was the first clue since then.

"I went there. I had trouble at first, but because of my resemblance to Christopher, finally one of the administrators talked to me. I didn't know what story he'd told, but I said we were separated by the courts, and he'd run away from a foster home. I explained that he wasn't always very truthful, but that if I could just see him, I was sure we could set everything straight. She was kind but firm. This was impossible; he had gone to a home, and without any papers to prove my claim, there was nothing she could do. Why didn't I have my social worker contact her? I don't know what she thought I was up to, but I don't think she believed me one bit.

"I left as if crushed, but she had invited me into her office, so I could go back. I returned that night, through a crack in her window frame, and read her files. I found out where he was, then I came here.

"I've been watching him, Zoë. I've seen what he does. You don't want to let him roam free in your town. He drinks their blood, Zoë."

"Like you?"

"But, Zoë, he doesn't have to kill them. Not like that."

"You've never killed anyone?" Her eyes were piercing.

Simon picked up his T-shirt and twisted it in his hands. "I told you I did. You know I did." Then he grabbed her hand. "But I don't have to. I can control it. He doesn't even try. He enjoys the kill."

Zoë took the T-shirt from him and smoothed it on her lap. "You can control it?"

"Yes, I've done it. I've lulled them into a gentle mist and sipped them slowly, then left them with breath."

He didn't mention the times he'd failed, when it had been so long since he'd tasted human blood that he couldn't pull away, and had fallen into that mist along with his prey, and floated there, awakening ages later with a cold empty shell in his arms. It was always more satisfying to the end, and he'd often wondered if his kind fed as much upon the dying as upon the blood. Christopher seemed to relish it more than the blood.

"What about that crucifix?" Zoë asked. "Was it hurting you?"

125

Simon

"Oh, no." He rubbed at his arm guiltily, as if it itched, an excuse to avert his eyes. "Just an old wives' tale. You can't believe everything you read. It was tasteless, that's all." What's wrong with me, he wondered. I thought I'd decided to trust her. Still, it felt frighteningly stupid to give someone a weapon against him.

"Simon?" Zoë touched his arm. "Where are your fangs?"

She looked as if she pitied him. Did she still think him a mad, hungry boy from the streets? "They can't just appear. They have to be stimulated by the smell or the promise of blood. Shall I show you?" he said half jokingly.

He reached for her and saw a spark of fear in her eyes. It excited him and urged him on. Ah, she believes just a little, he thought. Yet she folded into him and laid her head on his shoulder. She stroked his arm. Sweet warmth. Sweet, searing heat.

"Poor Simon. What can I believe?"

Her throat throbbed with life near his mouth, and the gentle, warm smell of her made him giddy. He fought it briefly, but it was no good; she was too near, too inviting. The fangs slid from their sheaths. "Believe this," he whispered, and kissed her neck softly. "And this, and this." Then he kissed her with the sharp, sleek kiss, the silver kiss, so swift and true, and razor sharp, and her warmth was flowing into him. He could feel it seeping through his body—warmth, sweet warmth.

Simon

She uttered a small, surprised cry and fought him for a second, but he stroked her hair and caressed her. I won't hurt you, he thought. Little bird, little dear. I won't hurt you. And she moaned and slipped her arms around him. It was the tender ecstasy of the kissed that he could send her with his touch. It throbbed through his fingers, through his arms, through his chest, like the blood through her veins. It thrummed a rhythm in him that he shared with her. She sighed, her breath came harder, and he felt himself falling. I must stop now, he thought. But I can't stop. He held her closer still, as if he could never let go. He couldn't let go.

Yet he did. Gasping, he firmly pushed her away. They stared at each other muzzily.

"I can stop if I want," he whispered hoarsely.

She blushed, then touched her neck and looked at the droplets of blood on her fingers wonderingly. "But it was . . . I mean, it wasn't terrible. It was . . . I don't know."

He wanted to kiss her again. "It can be terrible. He makes it terrible. I can make it sweet." He took her hand, and the throbbing began deep inside him once more. I can stop, he thought as he reached for her.

The phone rang. They both jumped.

Zoë pushed him away and went to answer it. "My mother," she said, almost apologizing.

He heard Zoë pick up the phone in the hall. She answered as if frightened, but then her tone changed to one

127

of surprise. "Lorraine! Hi! You did? She told you? Uh-huh. Yeah." There was hesitancy in her voice. "Yeah, I guess I was." Was that relief? "No, I was busy. Yeah. Trick-or-treaters." Her voice was warmer, as if she was ready to talk much more, but she must have remembered him. "Listen, I've got something to finish up. Can I call you back later? Okay. Bye." She hung up.

When she came back into the room, he could see the spell of the moment was gone. But what puzzled him was why she had panicked when she answered the phone. She must have guessed his thoughts. Her lips tightened, her gaze lowered. "I thought it might be about my mother," she said. "She's dying."

It was a terse confession, perhaps in return for his own rambling tale. They were sharing deaths, he thought with bitter humor.

"Listen," she said, "I think you should leave. I don't know when my father will be home. I couldn't explain you. It will be hard enough to explain this." She pointed at the table.

"You dropped something on it?" he suggested.

"Good grief, what? A bomb?"

Still, he wouldn't let her push him out so fast. "You'll let me come again?"

"Why?" Her hand went to her throat.

It made him feel ashamed. He stooped to pick up his T-shirt. "To talk," he muttered. "Just to talk."

"What have we to talk about?" It sounded like a denial.

He took a stab in the dark. "Death," he said.

Her eyes grew large and stricken, but she nodded. "Yes."

He couldn't stop the grin. He covered it by pulling on his shirt. "I'll come again—soon. Zoë, I didn't know I needed this so much." He grabbed her and gave her a quick, fierce kiss.

But it awoke bitterness once more. He was a failure at even this mockery he'd become. He'd spent years thinking of them as mindless, stupid creatures unfit to live, to make it easier to use them; now he had let one become real to him. What am I going to do? He thought. I won't be able to hunt again. He'd shrivel and twist but never die—and always the awful hunger. The idea of himself wasted and quite mad, crawling through some back alley somewhere, made him shudder.

She touched his face, her unbearably human eyes showing more concern than he'd ever deserved. "What's wrong?"

"I'll never get my revenge," he said. "Christopher is too clever for me. I might as well run away while I can and hide from *him*. Make some kind of a worthless life for myself elsewhere. I've always been a fool. A failure. He'll keep on killing and keep on evading me. He'll win."

"No. He can't." He was surprised by the quick spark of fire in her.

He tucked the portrait back under his arm and flung his jacket over his shoulder. She walked him to the door. "He will win, you know, because even if I kill him, I'll go on living endlessly, futilely, hating every unnatural second."

"Don't talk that way," she said. "You deserve more."

"No, I don't."

She let out a small cry of protest, of pain.

"Sorry. Till later, then."

She closed the door slowly, as if afraid to trust him to his own despair; then he was out in the dark again.

He slipped through the streets to his den, trying to sort out what he felt. The scruffy youth who began to follow him near the park was a minor problem. He lost the boy fast through the dark backyards.

At the light of dawn he curled in a dusty corner, and abandoned thought for the musky sleep that tasted of blood.

· 11 ·

Zoë

Zoë sat in the moonlight that slid molten through her window. It lay pooled on the pillow where her head had been minutes before. The silver light had pierced her eyelids as if they were transparent, keeping her from sleep.

They say people who sleep in moonlight become lunatics, she thought, and smiled. But it's too late, she added. I already am.

She curled her legs up to hug them with her arms, feeling the window-seat cover bunch beneath her, cotton daisies from a long-ago spring. The lawn outside sparkled with frost, and the whole night was diamond and fairy.

She thought of Simon. He'd held her so carefully, and his kisses had been so sweet that she'd wanted more. He had laced her neck with shivers. She barely noticed it when his fangs pierced her throat; except then it felt like

131

silver bubbles started to rise from her breast and burst within her head like champagne, and her body responded, surprising her into quickened breath. She blushed to think of how she had pulled him close. What was I saying to him? she wondered. It was like I was drunk.

I should be disgusted, she thought. But no, it wasn't disgusting now that she thought of it, but it was frightening. You could rush into your death unknowing, inviting, enjoying the ecstasy of it, burned up in bright light like a moth. She hadn't wanted him to stop.

Was it something Simon did on purpose, she wondered, or was it part of the disease, a compensation for the victim like the numbing poison of a spider's bite? Yet Christopher liked to feel his victim's fear. My God, she thought. If Simon can control the senses like that, what does Christopher do to them? The air of the room grew icy, and she pulled her robe closer around her.

What Simon had done was hard to believe at first, but there was the blood she had wiped from her throat, and the puncture wounds on her neck that had healed so fast. They had sealed in a matter of hours to leave just a bruise. She was still groggy and weak but strangely stimulated.

He had grown hotter and hotter as he drank from her warmth, and he had trembled. That trembling had aroused her as much as anything. She'd caused it. And he had stopped, hadn't he? She could trust him. Despite her doubts it was his loneliness that convinced her of that finally. He

Zoë

just needs someone to talk to, she thought, that's all, like me.

A dark shape in the yard below caught her eye, and her heart thumped. But it was just a cat, passing through. What was I afraid of? she thought. A small boy, perhaps, creeping up on my house?

But why was Simon afraid of Christopher? What could Christopher do to Simon that Simon couldn't do to him? Why was Simon giving up? Stop being a wimp, she wanted to shout at him as anger flashed through her. You can *do* something about *your* problem.

She eased her clenched fists. God, it was so dumb getting mad at someone who wasn't even there. But then, she'd been angry a lot lately. "Uh-oh," she breathed softly. She'd forgotten to call Lorraine back. I'll have to do it tomorrow, she thought, then sighed. She'd be wiped out tomorrow if she didn't get some rest. She rubbed her eyes and tried to feel sleepy. I better go back to bed, she decided.

She pulled the curtains against the disturbing light.

A steady gray rain beat down on the taut skin of Zoë's umbrella as she splashed her way to the bus stop. Each puddle caused the damp to creep farther up the legs of her corduroys, stiffening them against her calves. Cars hushed by, their drivers oblivious to the spray of water they sent splattering the sidewalk, their rear lights leaving streamers of red in the slick black street. Over the sidewalk the streetlamps misted the air with fractured light.

Her mother mustn't have known it was raining this hard. She never would have called if she knew Zoë would have to rush outside on a night like this, but the phone call had come, the one Zoë longed for but seldom received nowadays. "Come visit me," the husky voice had said. "Your dad's working tonight. I'll be lonely." Zoë had flung on her mother's London Fog raincoat, grabbed the red umbrella from the hall stand, and ran out into the night, barely taking time to check if she had bus fare in her pants pocket. Who cares about rain, she thought, grinning. She felt like a different person, miles from the girl who had been too tired to go to school today.

Then a spatter of footsteps from behind echoed someone running. They drew closer, fast. She stopped before she could help it, more curious than fearful. She turned just as the runner reached her.

"Zoë," Simon said, pulling up short, and he held out his hand.

A detached part of her wondered at his not being out of breath, while she took his hand automatically, as if she had been doing it for years. They continued walking, and she shifted the umbrella to cover him, too, but he didn't seem to notice.

"Where are you going?" He flipped his sopping-wet hair back from his eyes, scattering drops down her cheek.

134

"The hospital."

His eyes registered surprise, concern perhaps. "You are ill?"

"No, my mother's there."

"Oh."

They stepped off the curb to cross the street. She saw him wince as he hopped across the stream in the gutter. "You all right?"

"Flowing water," he explained. "It's a problem to me."

"What do you mean?"

"Water rejects the dead. A corpse floats to the surface, no matter how long it takes."

I can't believe I'm having this conversation, she thought. It's creepy.

"I am at odds with nature," he continued. "And the whole natural world tries to remind me of this. The sun burns me; and when I cross running water, I can feel it trying to heave me off the face of the earth. It makes me sick to my stomach."

No wonder he was sick on that voyage from England, she thought. If it's true. She squeezed his hand, and that made him smile.

They reached the bus stop, and he took in the red-and-white transit sign. "Can I come?" He dropped her hand to search his pockets but seemed to find nothing that satisfied him.

Zoë

"I have enough for you too," she said. Let him come. It felt right.

His hands stopped searching and relaxed into the side pockets of his jacket. "You don't mind sharing the time with her?"

"No." She was touched by his insight. "It'll be good for her. She doesn't get out much nowadays. She likes unusual people. She'll have a wonderful time trying to figure you out."

"You love her very much." It wasn't a question. "It's a difficult time for you."

"Understatement." Her lips twisted wryly.

"I haven't seen much of natural death. What is it your mother is dying of?"

Zoë bristled. How could he sound so cold? "She has cancer. I wouldn't call that natural."

"Sorry, I didn't mean to sound callous, but next to the death I've seen dealt, it seems much more natural. I mean, within the laws of nature at least."

The bus came. Zoë climbed the steps, folding her umbrella, and slammed enough change for both of them in the slot. He talked as if her mother were a specimen. She didn't bother to check if he followed her. She sat halfway down the almost empty bus, opposite the rear door, and laid the wet umbrella on the floor. When she sat up, she saw him grab the back of the seat in front and swing in gracefully beside her. He looked worried.

Zoë

"I didn't mean to trivialize your mother's death. I know it matters. Every death matters."

They were silent for a while, as the bus lurched through the night.

"At first," he finally said, "you think—no, hope—it might be a dream. That you'll wake up, and it will have been just a nightmare."

Zoë turned sharply to look at him. Was he mocking her? But his gaze was far away, not even on her.

"You think she'll be there," he continued, "pulling the curtains to let in the sun, wishing you good morning."

"Yes, how did you know?"

His eyes snapped into focus, catching the light like broken glass. "What kind of a son would I be, not to know?"

She blushed stupidly and couldn't seem to find a natural position for her hands to settle in. He'd lost his mother too. "Yes, of course."

"You forgot," he said in a gentler voice.

She nodded, embarrassed. "But I felt that way, too, or like maybe it was a cruel joke, and everyone would confess to it real soon."

"And then the anger," he said, as if it were inevitable. "Anger at her for going away."

"For ruining our lives," she joined in.

"At God," he said.

Zoë

"At everyone around, for not understanding, for not having it happen to them."

Simon nodded. "At myself, too, for not having been old enough at the time to understand, or perhaps to save her."

"I thought sometimes, I'm being punished," Zoë said, "but I didn't know what for. I started looking for things to do to atone."

A woman near the front of the bus turned to look at them, and Zoë realized the conversation had gotten louder. She lowered her voice. "Now I think, there's no payoff, no matter how good you are. No one's going to reward you. It's not like getting good grades in school—there's no logic, no prizes."

He sighed. "It pains me to hear you speak like that. So young, and so bitter."

She was surprised. "But what about you? After all this time, after all you've been through?"

"Yes, I suppose, but I've had much longer to become that way, and even then, isn't the point to do what's right for its own sake, even if there is no reward?" He gave a short snort of laughter. "But what am I talking about? What do I know of right and wrong? I've had to rationalize the wrong for so long, I'm not sure I could know the difference. It appears self-preservation is the strongest motivator of all—for everyone."

Zoë noticed that they were passing the hospital. "Damn!"

138

Zoë

She leapt for the bell cord. The bus ground to a halt at the stop by the farthest entrance, and they scrambled to get off. At least the rain had stopped; a piece of luck, since she'd forgotten the umbrella.

On the way up the long driveway he put his arm around her. He should be dead, she thought, three hundred years ago, and yet he's here comforting me. It doesn't make sense.

"Zoë," he said when they were halfway there, "don't let the anger make you push people away. Don't take it out on the people who love you. I cut myself off from my father, and look what happened to me. It tortures me to think of how it could have been. I should have recognized the form his grief took and comforted him. We could have stood against Christopher together. We could have won. I was a fool."

Zoë hugged him closer to her. "We don't ever have the benefit of hindsight in our decisions, let alone three hundred years' worth." Secretly she thought, Am I pushing them away? No, it's them. But his words nagged at her; she still hadn't phoned Lorraine.

As they neared the building, Simon slowed down. He tipped his head to examine its height like Jack facing the giant. She hesitated at the large glass doors. Would anyone really want to sit at the deathbed of someone he didn't even know? "Are you sure you want to come in?" she asked.

Zoë

"Yes," he said, but he looked frightened, unsteady.

"You could wait outside."

"No."

It didn't look as if he was going to move, however, so she went in ahead of him. He followed her and kept close like a child at the dentist. His eyes flicked rapidly here and there. She was sure a sudden noise would give him a heart attack—if that was possible. He almost flinched when someone passed him in the corridor. They drew a few curious stares, but this *was* a hospital. They probably think I'm taking him to the psych ward, she decided.

"I'm not used to the light," he said by way of excuse.

When the elevator doors closed, she wished for his sake they had taken the stairs. She could feel his panic like vibrations in the air. Thank goodness they were in there alone, because she didn't think he could have taken a crowd.

"The problem is," he said—and she could hear the click of his tongue in his dry mouth—"in my line of work you like to have an escape route." He cut short a nervous giggle by biting his lip.

Zoë smiled politely at the plump nurse at the fifth-floor station. The nurse smiled back. "Which room?"

"Five twelve."

"Oh, yes, Mrs. Sutcliff. She said she was expecting her daughter."

"That's me."

Zoë

"Well, go ahead, dear. I expect you know the way."
She looked doubtfully at Simon but held her tongue. He
stared back at her, a defiant young punk, his defense
mechanisms at work again.

Zoë tugged at his sleeve. "Come on." What was he up
to? Was he going to make a scene?

He broke eye contact with practiced indifference. Quite
an actor, she thought, remembering his distress only mo-
ments before. She could hear the nurses in the staff room
now—"It's the stress," they'd say. "It brings out the
devil in them. She's hanging out with hoods to get attention." It made her smile. If only they knew.

The smile faded when she came to her mother's door
and got no response to her gentle knock.

The lights were low, and her mother just a huddled
lump in the bed. A surge of terror made her rush to
the bedside, but the steady movement of breathing
quelled her fears. She lowered herself to a chair. Her
mother's slippers lay half under the bed, looking flat and
empty. I guess there won't be any conversation tonight,
she thought.

Simon, liquid with ease in the muted light, pulled a
chair up beside her. He looked at her mother with interest,
all the nervousness smoothed from his face. "Hence your
beauty," he said.

"But she's not like she was."

"I can still tell."

Zoë

She wasn't sure how to answer, so didn't.

I could shake her, she thought. I could wake her up. She almost reached out, but her mother looked so peaceful. Zoë crushed beneath her thigh the hand that wanted to touch. Let her sleep, she argued. She needs it. She has to grab what she can. But Zoë's lips were tight with disappointment. Why did she call if she was tired? I thought she wanted me here.

Simon gazed steadily at her mother's face. It was impossible to guess his thoughts. They made a strange pair: the dying and the undead. Is he wishing he could die too? she wondered. Is life forced on him as much as death is forced on her?

A thought suddenly struck her. Could he change her? Could he give her his blood like Christopher had given his? Surely they could find a way to get her the blood she would need without killing anyone. She would have time for her art, time for her family, all the time in the world. But would he do it?

"Simon," she whispered, "if a sick person became a vampire, would he heal?"

He twisted to look at her, horror on his face. "Would you wish that on someone?"

"Just tell me," she begged.

"Since I was changed, I have remained a youth—never growing, never aging. Wounds I have sustained since then have always healed rapidly. They repair and leave me as I was before." He tried to keep his voice low, but anger grew as he spoke, strangling his words. "If someone were to change with cancer in his body, the body would not alter too much, I think. The cancer would still be there, but the body would heal itself as fast as the cancer ate it away. In effect, that person would probably be in pain forever. What would that do to a person's mind, do you think?"

Zoë stifled a cry with her fist. Tears started to her eyes.

His voice softened. "The change can do terrible things to a person, Zoë. It's unnatural. Look at Christopher. At least I was allowed to grow up first, but he's trapped forever in the body of a child, and has a child's anger. His body whispers to him the secrets he will never know, because he can't quite hear them. I think that's why he kills so brutally. I could never turn anyone into something like that deliberately."

He was right. She knew he was right, but it had seemed a last gleam of hope, and now it was gone, almost as soon as she'd thought of it. And there he was, throwing Christopher at her again. "If he's so terrible, why don't you stop him?" she snapped.

It took him aback. "But I've tried."

His urgent, hushed tones reminded her to lower her voice. "So try again."

They argued in fierce whispers.

"He's stronger than me. He always outsmarts me."

"What are you frightened of? The fact he's your older brother? You're bigger than him; surely you're stronger than him?"

Simon clenched his fists. "What makes you so concerned with my problems?" he hissed.

"Your problems?" Zoë rose to her feet without realizing it. "You came to me, remember? You made me concerned. But it's not just your problem—it's everyone's problem. You'll be stopping him from killing others. Christopher brings death. This is death." She stabbed a finger in her mother's direction. "You can stop death."

Her mother groaned and stirred, and Zoë's breath left her for a moment. Had Mom woken? Had she heard? But her mother's body took on the rhythm of sleep once more, and Zoë relaxed. She sat down again.

Simon pulled the sheet up and carefully replaced it around the sleeping woman, as gently as if tucking it around his own lost mother. Death had taken her, too, Zoë remembered. No, not death, Christopher. "You've got to stop him, Simon. For your mother's sake."

He stared at his hands. "I'm afraid, Zoë. He could kill me. He knows how to do it."

Zoë was astounded. "You're afraid of death?"

Simon shrugged. "It doesn't matter how long you live, the idea of nonexistence is still frightening. No matter how tired you are of life, it's better than facing the unknown."

"But you don't have to lose." She glanced at her

mother. She couldn't fight the death taking her mother, but she could fight the death that had taken his. She could fight Christopher. "What if I helped?"

It was his turn to be astounded. "You'd help?"

"Yes, because I know you can do it."

He reached to stroke her hand. "How can I let you endanger yourself?"

"Let me help you," she said, "or I swear I'll do it myself." And at that moment she felt she could.

He laughed suddenly, his eyes lighting up. "I have never received such an offer." His voice was tender. "How could I ever fail with you beside me?"

"We'd better go," she said, already frightened at her own words. "I've got a phone call to make."

Before they left, she took a folded piece of paper from her coat pocket, smoothed it out, and laid it under her mother's hand. It was a poem—"Spells against Death."

· 12 ·

Simon

It was too cold for lovers, and too late. A chill November night wind rustled the bushes, rattling azaleas, making the privets hiss. But Simon didn't feel the cold—ice kissing ice doesn't freeze—neither did he sweat as he thrust the stolen shovel repeatedly into the hard-packed soil. The lip of the trench was already at his knee.

The leather coat lay across a branch. One arm of the jacket swung drunkenly each time a load of dirt hit the trunk of the shrub that held it. Simon's muscles bunched and strained in relentless rhythm as he tore a gash in the earth.

Clouds covered the sky, but he didn't need light to see by, even if the witch's moon was high enough to help. He had animal eyes, and the steady pace of his work was the gait of the wolf, who could run all night till it found its prey.

Simon

The hole came to his waist. He thought of Zoë as he dug, and the pleasure of it spurred him on—the torture of her skin, her human breath, the shadows in her eyes, her fragile bones, the whole ephemeral beauty of her that would fade and die before he'd ever wear one wrinkle on his face. I could cup one of those sweet breasts, he thought, and she'd be gone, before ever the pleasure had stopped singing in me.

He mustn't let himself care. He'd spend longer missing her than knowing her. But was it a wonder that he'd lasted this long without caring, or was it a wonder that he could care at all? Who knew? He chuckled softly at the thought that age brought knowledge. It just brought new surprises.

It was sad that Zoë's mother was dying, and sadder that Zoë already missed her. I could tell her, *It's not too bad*, he thought. *Your life is short. It's not a long time to miss someone.* But she wouldn't believe him. It was all she had. A lifetime was a lifetime, regardless of its years.

The hole was deep enough. It was ragged and uneven, but deep enough. He yanked the corner of a moth-eaten blanket above him and rolled the waiting bundle down. The finishing touches didn't take long. He threw the shovel out and then, with preternatural strength, leapt after it, defying gravity. He grunted fiercely at the pleasure it still brought.

How much sadness have I caused? he wondered as he arranged scavenged branches across the pit. Were they missed as badly, the people I took to extend my worthless

147

life? He had never thought of them as being missed by someone. He'd thought of the cruelty of taking their lives, he'd worried at the pain they might feel, but it never entered his head that there would be pain left behind. How stupid I am, he thought. Am I doomed to be a shallow youth forever, as Christopher is a petulant child? What a waste of years, never learning from them, never growing. It was all so senseless, but all part of the same curse.

He spread the blanket on the branches and began covering it with the dead leaves that clogged the lower joints of the bushes.

The moist, pungent smells brought back to him another autumn, the one when he had found his way back to his father's house, too late. He had peered through the diamond panes, like a thief, at a wizened, white-haired man, who wore grief and pain on his face like a web. There was no one there to comfort the old man as he tossed and turned on his bed, no son to hold his dying hand. A servant brought in a drink to the nightstand, turned down the light, and left, never speaking once.

Simon had stood there all night, his face pressed to the glass. There was no one to invite him in. He could only wait and stare longingly at his father, aware that even if fate gave him a door, he could never enter, never tell his father what he had become. Better to let him suffer in ignorance than in the unbearable pain of knowing both his sons damned.

Trapped on the other side of the window, trapped in the

world of the night, Simon knew they were forever separate now, no matter who it was alive, or dead, or dying.

He left before the sun rose, his heart as swollen with grief as if it were beating. He had barely stopped being an animal and remembered he had been human once, when he was forced to put aside that knowledge, deny that heart to stop the pain.

He stayed close in London, though he never dared look again, and when he heard of his father's death it was money robbed from a drunk that bought the family portrait from a skulking, thieving footman, not three hours past the burial. The only ones he could love were now dead. He could never care for someone again, and no one would ever care for him.

But Zoë cares, he thought as he tossed a last handful of leaves on the pile. She said she'd help me. No one has ever helped me; yet, knowing what I am, she'll help. He moved a broken trellis and began shoveling earth into the damp hole behind. Yes, there were still surprises.

As the sky silvered, before the red sun tore shreds in the east, Simon approached the boarded window of his den. It was there he received a different surprise—nasty.

It slammed into his chest—fear—knocking the stolen breath from him. A sheet of paper fluttered on the wooden slats, impaled with a pin, white as a corpse. He ripped it away with trembling fingers and read the clumsy print.

I know where you are.

Simon

Simon's fingers tightened convulsively, ripping a corner off. He fumbled for the letter, reading on.

> I am tired of this game. You bore me. I can follow you, and you'll never know. I can kill you, and you won't have a chance. No more cat and mouse. No more nice to brother. You are a pest, a gnat. No one will miss you. No one will notice. No one will care. Run, Simon, run. You are dead.

It was signed *Christopher*.

"Too late," Simon muttered, "too late," and crushed the note in his hands. It stopped them from shaking. Maybe last week I'd have run, he thought, but not now. I have a weapon you don't know about, Christopher. Then his eyes widened with an awful thought. Zoë! Did he know about Zoë? Simon suddenly wanted to run to her, warn her. Or should he run *away*, hide, never go near her again? He turned, indecisive, almost in panic, and saw the horizon tinged pink. I can't go anywhere, he realized with a sinking dread. There's nothing I can do. I'm trapped again by my own stinking disease.

He yanked a board away to get inside and slid through, ripping his jeans on a nail.

But he can't go out, either, Simon comforted himself, not unsupervised, not during daylight. Christopher was as trapped as he was, and even if he should reach her, he hadn't much strength under the sun. Then another thought

Simon

struck him. "I'm a fool," he said, and slapped the board carelessly into place behind him. *No one will miss you,* Christopher had written. *No one will notice.* He didn't know about her.

But when had Christopher followed him? Had it been the night after Simon's botched attack, or one of the subsequent nights? Simon ran his fingers through his fine hair repeatedly, unconsciously, sweeping it back from his face. If only he knew. But surely, if Christopher had seen him with her, he'd throw it in his face, threaten her to taunt him? That would be like Christopher. Yes, he thought, sinking down in relief, that would be much more like him. *So he followed me a night I didn't see her, or found me after,* Simon decided. *He really doesn't know she exists.*

Simon dragged the suitcase out from under the desk and stroked the surface carefully, drawing strength from his native earth. *I will sleep,* he thought. *I will sleep and get strength. And then we will see.*

But the fear still plagued him as he tried to take his rest. *What if I'm wrong? What if he knows, and he's leading me on? What if he hurts her?*

Tortured by his thoughts, he didn't see the first burning ray of sun slide through the crack where the board didn't fit.

· 13 ·

Zoë

She was outside Lorraine's house. They were bringing a stretcher out. Zoë's mother was on it, eyes closed, face pale, but she spoke. "I forgot my painting. Can you get it? I have to take it with me." They carried her where an ambulance waited. Zoë wanted to get the painting for her mother before they left. She walked through the hospital doors.

The elevator was small. A metal grid clamped shut with an echoing crash as she stepped inside. She was trapped. The elevator shook violently as it climbed—slowly, agonizingly slowly. Hurry up. Hurry up. She didn't recognize any of the floors it opened on. The lift ground to a halt, but the doors were jammed. Slats began to fall from the floor one by one. Fear clenched in her throat. She pounded the metal, begging it to relent. She was going to fall, to crash down floor after floor and end up a limp puppet on basement concrete.

Zoë

The doors opened, but the elevator hadn't quite reached the floor. She struggled for footholds up the brick wall and crawled through the crack, her breath ragged. Blinding white light greeted her.

She was on a ledge high above the street. The ambulance, far below, was leaving. "Don't go!" Stomach-wrenching fear would allow her only to crawl on her belly along the ledge, clutching its sides against the great empty rushing space below. The wind screamed above her.

She swung her legs over the edge. She had to catch up. At first there was nothing except the certainty of plunging death. Great chunks of building began to fly off at her hands' touch. Her toes found wall. Her feet scrambled and slipped. She slid and cried out, expecting to meet the sidewalk abruptly, but found a handhold again. Scraped and gashed, she reached the ground.

The ambulance was still leaving. She ran after it. Her legs wouldn't move fast enough, as if the air were thick. Tears ran down her face.

Lorraine was beside her, and she offered Zoë a painting. Zoë burst with anger and hit her. "It's all right," Lorraine said. "She's only going to Oregon. You can visit."

A wave of relief washed over Zoë. She took the painting. In it was a boy with silver hair, dressed in bright colors, laughing.

Zoë lay blinking in the pale dawn light coming through the bedroom curtains. She moved her head slightly to make sure Lorraine was still on the floor in her sleeping

Zoë

bag. The dream clung to her like a mist. She's only going to Oregon. You can visit. She could still feel the relief. I was angry at Lorraine, she thought. I was getting them mixed up—both going away. It's not her fault, not the fault of either of them. I might have been taking it out on her.

She studied Lorraine's sleeping face. I have to memorize it, she thought.

Around the green sleeping bag, where Lorraine snuggled on the floor, were scattered photographs, yearbooks, diaries, homemade picture books, and Zoë's notebooks full of poetry; the accumulated memories of years of friendship. The turntable still circled lazily. They had forgotten it completely as they lay in bed talking long after the last record had been played.

Lorraine was leaving today. That's what made it different from the many other mornings they had shared. Thank God I called her, Zoë thought. We wouldn't have had even this. I didn't realize it was creeping up so fast.

Lorraine had seemed tentative last night, at first—almost shy, not like her. She seemed eager to please. Maybe I should have got mad at her more often, Zoë thought perversely, and not let her walk all over me.

"You look pale," Lorraine had said soon after arriving. "You're not ill, are you?"

Zoë had smiled at her friend's concern. The attention felt good. "No. It's just . . . things, I guess."

"Geez, just things." Lorraine shook her head. "And I

154

thought you were supposed to be the articulate one." But the sarcasm in her voice didn't match the way she behaved— unsure if she should take her things up, asking to use the bathroom—almost like she'd never spent the night before.

I never thought of her as insecure, Zoë thought, but I snap at her, and she acts like I might dump her for good.

Zoë found herself trying to reassure Lorraine in small ways, dumb ways, really, like chuckling if she said something even slightly funny, or letting her decide what they should make for dinner, and soon Lorraine got her sea legs again. She happily bullied Zoë into helping her concoct a huge pot of spaghetti and made her eat a large helping of it, all the while complaining of how fat she was getting.

"Bull," Zoë said. "You've got a great figure, not like me."

Lorraine sniffed. "You might be skinny, but your bra's bigger than mine. You better eat more, otherwise every time you get up, you'll fall over from the weight of your tits."

They screamed with laughter at this image until they had to wipe tears from their eyes.

They were getting ready to clear the dishes away when Harry Sutcliff came home. Lorraine flirted with him outrageously, as usual, and cajoled him into eating too. Zoë felt warmed by the way he actually smiled a little, and tucked in with more appetite than she had seen in him for a while. It's Lorraine, she thought. There's so much life in her, it's catching. Zoë didn't feel as worried as she might have when he excused himself quietly and disappeared to his bedroom with a briefcase of work to catch up on, but he never came out to ask them to quiet down as he might have once. Zoë didn't know whether to be relieved or irritated. She kept on half expecting to hear his voice.

They had stayed awake long past the time when things made sense, as if fighting off the inevitable by making the night last forever. They pigged out on chips and dip, listened to records, and giggled at stupid jokes as if they were at a fifth-grade slumber party all over again.

Yet there were awkward silences sometimes, when they strayed too close to dangerous ground.

Finally, Lorraine tried to talk about her mother. She stumbled over her words. "It's not fair. I was just getting used to having to go somewhere else to visit her, and now I'll hardly ever be able to do that even." She cut herself short and messed around with a pile of albums as if looking for something.

Zoë knew it was the specter of her own mother's death between them, stopping Lorraine from venting all her fears, and she sighed. I sometimes think she's selfish, but she's not, not really, Zoë realized. It *is* unfair for her. She deserves to feel bad. She's losing her mother too. The last took Zoë by surprise. She'd been so wrapped up in herself that she'd never thought about it that way.

"Lorraine," she said softly, in one of the silences when she could bear it no longer, "I'm sorry I'm such a jerk."

Lorraine threw a bottle top at her. "You said that last

night." But she looked warily at Zoë, sensing more to come.

"But I'm still a jerk if you can't talk to me. I'm not going to shatter and break if you talk about your mother. I'm sorry if I've been a self-centered pig, and made you feel that way." She felt her face glowing with embarrassment.

Lorraine turned away.

God, I've pissed her off, Zoë thought, confused. Lorraine's shoulder's were shaking. No, worse. She'd made her cry. Zoë slid from her bed and crawled across to her friend, unsure of what to do next. I have to be tactful, she thought, just as her hand came down firmly in the bacon-and-chive dip.

"Ugh!"

Lorraine looked around, tears in her eyes, saw Zoe's hand, and howled—with glee. It was impossible not to join in.

"You'll either have to wash it or lick it," Lorraine gasped between giggles. "Here, have some chips."

"Shut up, you'll choke."

Gales of laughter again.

On her way to the bathroom Zoë said, "I guess we can talk now, huh?"

Lorraine took a deep breath. "I guess."

But there was one thing Zoë couldn't talk about.

What could I say? she thought at one point. There's this cute boy, and he likes to drink blood? She'll think I've gone round the bend.

Zoë

Often her fingers strayed to her neck and stroked the fading marks. It had been three nights; the wounds had healed fast. They were just pale yellow bruises now. She'd said she'd help him, but how could she do that? What had possessed her to say it? It was his kisses. What if it were all a mistake? What if someone innocent got dreadfully hurt?

She tossed and turned, unable to sleep even after Lorraine had been snoring for what seemed like hours.

But now it was morning, and the first shaft of sunlight lit Lorraine's hair, bringing out hidden gold in the rioting tendrils. It could have been Lorraine down that alley, if Simon was right. Wasn't that reason enough to help him? She tried to hold on to the moment and push that thought aside. It will always be like this, Zoë thought, hard as a wish. It will never change. This is every morning Lorraine has lain asleep on my floor, and I'll be within those mornings, never ceasing, from now on. There is no sad vampire boy, with sharp kisses, waiting out there in the cold somewhere.

Then Lorraine uncurled, and her eyelids fluttered. She stretched to grasp the day, and time moved on.

It was the last time they would toss for the shower, the last time they would decide together what to wear, the last time Lorraine would snitch a spray of Zoë's favorite cologne, and the last time they would try to outmaneuver each other for the best view in the mirror. Well, it wasn't really. They would visit each other, of course, but somehow that wasn't the same. Although, Zoë couldn't help but think, if Christopher had his way, they wouldn't even have that. She shuddered.

Lorraine made scrambled eggs and bacon for breakfast. She sang as she cooked, as if the unburdening of her worries had released the music in her.

"You're going to make someone an obnoxious wife someday," Zoë said.

Harry Sutcliff walked into the kitchen, sniffing the air, and sat down at the table. "I'm surprised you found anything here to cook."

Lorraine laughed. "I didn't. I brought this with me. Someone had to clean out the fridge."

"Well, you're a great cook," he said, pulling a plate of toast toward him.

Lorraine passed him the butter. "It's survival. You know Diane can't cook squat. Anyhow, the way to a man's heart, you know. I'm practicing my skills on you." She winked at him.

Zoë was amazed to see her father blush. He smiled shyly down at his plate and looked years younger. Such a small thing, Lorraine's flirting, yet it lightened his heart for a moment. Perhaps it was a glimpse of the boy Mom had fallen in love with that she saw. If I could learn to make him smile, she thought, it would be easier for us.

He left right after he ate, because he wanted to get some work in before he went to the hospital. The girls lingered over the cleanup. "He works so hard," Lorraine said.

Zoë

"Yeah. Bills, bills, bills." Zoë's voice was gentle. She felt more compassion for the man she had seen a glimmer of this morning, different from the rigid stranger who had been around for weeks.

Lorraine washed while Zoë wiped dry. Their last minutes ticked away, and Zoë still held a secret from her closest friend.

This is my last chance, she thought. But what do I say? Lorraine, there's this vampire, and I said I'd help him kill his brother, who happens to be a vampire too? It's that little boy you talked to. He almost murdered you. Oh, no, I don't know how we're going to do it. I've left that up to him. If I tell her that, she'll freak.

What could Lorraine do, anyway? She was leaving today. She couldn't tell Diane not to go—not for that reason. Diane would have them both locked up. Lorraine would worry herself sick all the way to Oregon. Zoë couldn't do that to her.

But what am I going to do when he comes back? she thought. Can I tell him I've changed my mind?

"Daydreaming, Zo?"

Zoë started. "I guess so."

"About a boy? Oh, don't look so surprised. I can tell a hickey when I see one."

Before she could help it, Zoë's hand went once more to her neck. She blushed. "I—"

"I know," Lorraine interrupted. "You met some cute boy, and before you knew it, you let him go and nibble your neck, even though you hardly knew him, and then you didn't tell me because you thought you were being slutty. I was biting my tongue all last night so I wouldn't ask. Honestly, Zoë, you'd think it was a crime. You only live once. Is he cute?''

Zoë nodded, afraid to speak.

"Are you seeing him again?"

"Yeah."

"Good grief, shut up. I can't bear to hear you run on at the mouth so much. Never mind. I'm just pissed you didn't tell me. But I know you. As soon as you've mulled it over long enough, you'll tell me—'cept you'll have to write this time." Lorraine suddenly looked solemn. "Promise you'll write, Zoë."

"Of course, silly." Zoë shook her friend's shoulder gently, relieved to change the topic. "Huge long, intricate letters about absolutely everything."

Lorraine sighed. "I can see I'll have to buy a dictionary."

"It's only Oregon," Zoë said, amused at her private joke. "I can visit."

They put away the last dishes, Lorraine collected her belongings, and they walked to Lorraine's house to meet Diane. They went slowly, hand in hand as they had done when they were eight years old.

When they got to the house, everything seemed to speed up. The car was almost fully packed, which Diane was glad to point out to Lorraine, Zoë noticed uncomfortably, but they helped to squeeze in the last few bags. Diane made a fuss about positioning her guitar safely, while Lorraine looked increasingly annoyed.

"The good thing is," she whispered to Zoë on the other side of the Toyota, "she can't play it while she's driving."

They scoured the echoing house for anything left behind and found nothing. Finally, they couldn't put it off any longer. Diane sat in the car, impatiently jangling her keys, and Lorraine had to get in beside her.

"We've got a long drive," Diane said. "Good-bye, Zoë. It's been nice knowing you."

Lorraine glared at her stepmother and grabbed Zoë's hand through the window. "I'll call as soon as I can."

Then the car was backing out of the driveway, turning onto the quiet suburban road, and heading for the highway. Zoë watched it disappear around the next corner. "GZN two five six," she intoned, as if witnessing a car escape from an accident.

She trailed home, turning her back on what would now always be "Lorraine's old house," and which she would never enter again. Alone, she thought. No, not quite. She had a date coming up. She smile dryly as she opened the front door and stepped into the silent house.

When her father returned home that night, he came to her room, where she was sitting in bed reading. Zoë smiled tentatively and patted her comforter. He accepted her invitation and sat, then he took a deep breath as if preparing himself for something that scared him. She tensed.

"I'm sorry about the other day," he said, rubbing his

chin nervously. "Your mother and I have been talking about it a lot. You're right. I haven't been giving you enough credit. After all, you've had to look after yourself so much lately, and you've done it and not complained. If that's not mature, I don't know what is. We just wanted to protect you, Zoë. But I've already said that."

Zoë was embarrassed that he was apologizing, yet she was glad. She wasn't quite sure what to do, however. She wanted a hug, but she felt too shy.

"I had a talk with this guy at the hospital. Your mom talked me into it. This therapist guy. Apparently they have these counseling sessions for families of—of . . . patients."

Zoë knew what he meant—terminally ill. But she still couldn't make herself say it.

"He made some sense; I was surprised, really. Don't know why. Thought I was the only one who ever went through it, I guess. But he really hit the nail on the head a few times, about how I was feeling, that is." He stared past her at the wall, as if it were easier to speak that way. "Anyhow"—his gaze shifted down to the carpet, still avoiding her eyes—"I thought you might like to come along next time. Next week, maybe. It might help us through this. I don't know. God knows, we need something. They've got groups. That sort of thing."

He rubbed at his corduroys nervously. She reached over to the fidgeting hand. Whoever this man at the hospital was, he seemed to have gotten through to her father. Maybe there was hope in this. "I'd like to give it a try."

He looked up and gave her a relieved smile. "That's settled, then." He brought his hand down on his knee like a judge's gavel. Then his smile faded slightly.

"She's not going to feel too good tomorrow. Another treatment. But we want you to come the next day, Zoë, and have a proper talk—about everything, everything you can think of. I think we all need it. You can stay as long as you like."

"I'd like that," she said, daring to feel relief.

He took her hand. "We don't want you to feel shut out. We never did."

Zoë squeezed his hand back. "I know, but—well—I've felt so rotten." She couldn't hold the tears back. Damn, she thought, I don't want to make him feel bad again. I don't want to scare him off.

But her father took her in his arms and held her, and stroked her back. He's really trying, she thought, and that made her cry harder. He was her daddy again. He would look after her and make things all right.

She was finally all cried out, and he pulled away. "Why don't you get some sleep." He kissed her forehead and left, closing the door.

Zoë turned out the bedside lamp and settled down to sleep. It should have been easier now, because she felt a weight was lifting from her. But she remembered Simon, and the weight came crashing down again. When is he coming back? she thought. What have I got myself into?

But her father was talking now, more open, so perhaps

he would understand. Maybe he could get her out of it somehow. No. If she didn't think Lorraine would believe her, why would her father? He has to believe, she thought. I don't lie. He'd at least believe she'd met a dangerous young man and do something about it. Call the police, maybe, and not leave her alone.

She talked herself out of bed, and to her father's door. She knocked lightly. No answer. She knocked again, a little louder. Still no answer. She opened the door and looked inside. He lay on the rumpled bedspread fully clothed and fast asleep. His briefcase lay beside him on the bed, unopened. He frowned in his sleep and snored slightly, an airy whistle like a child's. He was exhausted. She realized how unfair it would be to tell him, how absurd to expect him to believe. I can't wake him, she thought, and returned to her room. It's up to me now.

She slept late the next day, and her father was gone when she woke; whether to the office to get a quiet Sunday's worth of work in or to the hospital, she didn't know. He'd forgotten to leave a note.

She spent some time reading, curled into an armchair in the den with a fat science-fiction book, part of a series. But often she found she had read the same paragraph over twice and still not understood it. Her thoughts kept on returning to the evening. Would he come tonight? Finally she gave up on reading and went down to the basement to throw some laundry in the washer, then she dragged out the vacuum cleaner.

Zoë

Toward evening she sat at the kitchen table with her notebook and a pen, molding an idea into a poem.

> At the heart of night
> watch for the lone boy
> waiting in the pale moon's light
> eyes forever changing ice to cloud
> Stars
> upon faded jeans
> upon silver hair
> black leather shines
> Half wild
> still slightly mad
> bewildered by time
> chained to the night
> As he stalks
> he might hear a sound
> shift into a moonbeam
> and be gone.

There was a scratching at the back door. She blinked, put down her pen, and turned to face the door. The small windows reflected back, yet she could see a shadow outside. The key inside turned impossibly, the lock popped, and the door opened silently, all by itself. Simon stepped from the night into her home.

"I only have to be invited once."

"You don't have to be quite so melodramatic," she snapped in relief.

Zoë

Looking abashed, he sat at the table and took the notebook from her. He read while she watched. I keep forgetting how beautiful he is, she thought with surprise.

"What if my father was here?" she asked.

"I knew you were alone." He smiled at her written words and touched her cheek with icicle fingers. "I've waited centuries for you."

For a moment she flirted with a picture of them fleeing hand in hand, away from the problems of the world. *Take the night*, a tiny voice whispered, but she shrugged it off.

"Have you got an idea of what to do?" She was dismayed to hear the tremble in her voice. She was hoping he hadn't.

Simon laid the notebook on the table. "I've got a plan."

She caught sight of his other hand, the hand he hadn't touched her with. He held it under the table. She reached for it, and he tried to withhold it from her, but gave in reluctantly. It was burned. A nasty red welt lay across it.

"I stayed out too long," he said simply.

"The sun?" she asked.

"I was in a hurry to get safe inside; a sleep was coming on. I didn't secure the boards over the window well enough, and the sun must have come through a crack. The pain woke me."

She made a sympathetic noise.

He grinned. "Yes, it hurts like hell, but it'll heal fast."

"But how does Christopher get away with pretending to be a real child if he can't go out in daylight either?"

Zoë

"We can stand a few weak morning rays, or a brief moment on a cloudy day. They think he's an albino. They bundle him up and keep him out of strong light, to protect his 'delicate' skin. He wouldn't like to try full sunlight, though." Simon smirked, as if enjoying that thought.

Albino. Zoë thought of the boy at the alley mouth again and shuddered. It *was* him. She grew angry. She couldn't let him threaten the life of another girl like Lorraine.

Simon took his hand from her and picked up her pen. "Can I use your book?"

She nodded. She felt firmer now that she'd decided.

He turned to a clean page and drew an octagon. "This is that little structure in the park."

"The gazebo," she muttered, and he nodded.

He drew an oblong on one side. "This is a pit on the opposite side from your bench. I dug it last night."

"But surely someone would notice it today?"

"I disguised it."

"Simon, what if someone fell in?"

"No one walks around that way. Hardly anyone would be playing there in this weather."

He seemed oblivious to the danger to innocents. It frightened her, because it made him less human. "Why a pit?"

"There are stakes at the bottom. I want you to lure him over them. They're very sharp. I think they'll do the job."

Her stomach roiled. "I always wondered why they worked. In the movies, I mean. When you're supposed to be invulnerable."

Zoë

"We have to be pierced right through," he said, looking uncomfortable himself. "Not just injured, impaled. It holds the unnatural body long enough for the soul to escape. The soul that's been trapped and kept in torment. Then there can be true death."

She wondered at the selfishness of a body that could imprison its own soul. What would it do to someone who threatened it? "What if he catches me?"

"I'll be there, Zoë. I won't let anything happen to you. I'll be watching. He won't suspect you, so you can lead him. If it were me, he wouldn't follow so blindly. If he catches on, I'll be out there like a flash to distract him. Get him to cross that patch of ground."

"But how will I get him to follow me?"

"We'll pass by his house. I know the time he leaves. He has to wait for the family to sleep. He'll follow you—beautiful and alone—I know it."

"When do we go?"

"Not for a few hours yet."

"That's a long time."

"I have some things to tell you, about the earth he needs, about his bear. Things that might help you. Anyway"—his voice became soft and eager—"I thought you might let me kiss you again."

She glanced away nervously, her hand flying to her throat.

"No," he whispered. "Just a kiss. A real kiss."

*   *   *

Zoë

While Zoë retrieved her coat from the banister, Simon stood at the front door, kicking at the frame. "Stop that," she said. "I'm nervous, too, you know."

He looked up as if forcing himself to do so. "There's a chance he might know about you," he said in a rush. He walked out.

She ran out after him, her nerve endings screaming. "What do you mean?"

He stood outside, head bent, hands shoved into his pockets. "I'll understand if you don't go."

She felt herself turning white. "You weren't going to tell me, were you?"

"No."

"What changed your mind?"

"Your damn kisses." He shoved a piece of paper at her.

She read the childlike prose, gradually becoming puzzled. "But, Simon, it says nothing about me."

"No, but he's a spiteful sort. It would be like him to let me think you're safe."

He's paranoid, that's all, she thought. He's reading things into it. And he did tell me. He couldn't go ahead without telling me, after all, even if he is desperate.

"You've got to put faith in yourself sometime," she said tenderly, despite the lump in her throat. "The chance is no greater than it was before, and I couldn't get more frightened."

At midnight she walked down the quiet street, dressed to lure.

Zoë

Simon was out there, she knew, watching her, keeping her safe. She had to believe he could keep her safe. Yet her palms were sweating, and her mouth was dry. She had hung the crucifix Lorraine had given her around her neck, under her sweater. It made her feel better, no matter what Simon said. It didn't hurt to cover all bases.

Her stockinged legs were cold, but she hugged her jacket around her and forced herself to walk slowly. She wanted to give him ample opportunity to spot her.

Zoë knew when Christopher started to follow her, though she never heard him. The texture of the air changed. Perhaps the part of Simon left in her blood could sense it.

She walked toward the park under a star-crazed, clear, cold night, hardly daring to breathe.

· 14 ·

Simon

Simon watched Zoë from the shadows. He slipped from tree, to bush, to fence, but always he kept his distance.

How pretty her legs are, he thought. How beautiful her long dark hair—like Bess in that poem about the highwayman. Yet he dropped that thought quickly, remembering how Bess died to save her love. It made him feel uncomfortable. She awoke poetry in him, though. "She walks in beauty," he whispered. He smiled. A car drove by slowly, and he faded into a mist.

She turned the corner, and he drifted across a lawn to follow. He felt fuzzy, as he always did when he dissolved. It was hard to maintain a purpose that way. I can't allow myself to drift tonight, he decided, and reached out his mind to draw his scattered molecules together, seamlessly condensing into a pale boy in graceful motion behind a trellis fence.

Then he knew Christopher was there, ahead of him. He couldn't see the boy at first, and he started to panic. Then a movement in the trees caught his eye—a bat, up where she wouldn't see. Bats used sonar. He cursed silently and drifted apart again. It wouldn't catch him now. I hope he doesn't stay that way long, Simon thought as the numb apathy began to build.

He sensed Zoë's pace quickening. She knows. Slow down. He'll guess. Slow down. The last thought echoed around him, and Simon began to slow himself, started to drift. Ah, the sparkling night. Why don't I drift up to the stars? No. I must follow. Follow who? The girl. What girl? I think I shall scatter and sparkle like frost. *No,* a voice of reason called distantly. *Christopher,* hissed a quiet memory. The warning ran from molecule to molecule and pulled them together with the same purpose. It molded him back into a boy.

He crouched by a parked Volvo. Around the bumper he could see the park across the street. Two boys passed, smoking cigarettes and punching each other with the blows of comrades. They disappeared around the corner. He had gotten ahead of Zoë, but he could see her coming up the other side of the street. He could only hope that Christopher had not sensed the suspicious mist drifting out of tune with the night.

If Zoë could lead Christopher into the park, all would be

well. If she could only get to the other side of the pit, stop as if dreaming, to lure him out and entice him to approach her. "Oh, poor little boy," she could say, and call him across the trap, to his death.

A dark form flittered beneath the streetlights over Zoë's head. She didn't look up, but Simon saw her flinch at the shadow cast on the sidewalk. Don't look. Don't let him know. Her fists were clenched tight, but she didn't even glance. Simon could hear the pipings Zoë couldn't, the high-pitched squeal that bounced through the air and felt out shapes and movement in the night. He dared not move, lest he attract Christopher.

Then the bat was ahead of Zoë. It dipped around a tree and disappeared. And, at the park, a small boy stepped from the bushes out onto the sidewalk. He carried a knapsack over his shoulder. A teddy bear poked its head out from under an unbuckled strap. The boy waited for Zoë with anticipation on his face.

Simon bared his teeth and growled softly at the back of his throat. Damn his eyes. He couldn't wait any longer? He couldn't follow her farther? Did he know?

Zoë reached the park, and Christopher walked up to her, the knapsack bumping his thigh. Zoë looked startled. Don't give it away, Simon begged. He's just a boy to you, remember. He raised a hand to his mouth and worried a nail. Damn! Damn! Damn!

They talked. Simon could not quite hear what they said, even with ears acutely tuned for the hunt. It was too far to make out words, and it nearly drove him crazy. Perhaps Christopher's words gave him away. Perhaps he did know her. Zoë wouldn't be able to tell, but Simon could—if only he could hear.

Zoë walked into the the park with Christopher, offering her hand. Good girl. Brave girl. Her smile looked strained to him, but Simon suspected Christopher did not care enough about humans to tell a false smile from a true.

Simon followed carefully at a distance as they traveled the path to the center of the park. It was the right direction, and he dared to hope. But they stopped in the dark of a wide-spreading tree. Not here, Simon pleaded silently. Don't stop here. The moonlight didn't penetrate the shadows, and he could only see shady forms. Don't look into his eyes, he thought. Remember what I said. He'll have you, if you do that. Get out of there. Get out. Yet they stayed there in the dark, as if in eternity, and Simon wanted to howl.

This was all wrong; he had to go to her. He took the risk and eased himself through the night. If I can get close, I can jump him, he thought.

The figures were clearer the closer he got, and he saw the small form hold up something to the girl. Then he was close enough to hear the chirping voice. "This is Teddy. He's lost too. Kiss Teddy and make it better."

Zoë bent to the child, closer and closer into the reach of those greedy hands. He would grasp her hair, expose her throat—he would have her. Simon tensed to spring.

"Oh, what a lovely bear," Zoë cried, and snatched the toy from Christopher. He tottered back a step, and Simon held motionless in shock. What was she doing?

"Gimme my bear," Christopher said, recovering.

Zoë held it out of his reach. "I'm just looking."

"Gimme my bear," Christopher said more forcefully.

She laughed. It sounded forced to Simon. "What's wrong? Can't take a joke?" She backed away a few steps, and Christopher advanced on her, his fists clenched.

"Give it back." He almost used the command tone but stopped short, still playing the helpless child.

"Come on, don't you want to play?" she asked, backing away faster. "If you want it, come get it." She turned and burst from the shadows, holding in front of her the bedraggled teddy bear.

Christopher let out a cry of rage and rushed out behind her, panic on his face.

Simon grinned and punched the air in glee. Go, Zoë, go. She just might do it. He wanted to cheer.

She headed toward the gazebo. "Come on," she called. "You're no fun."

Simon felt like laughing. Christopher didn't dare go lightning fast and grab it back, because that would give his game away. He still thought he had a chance. He didn't know. He played the helpless little boy, running after his beloved teddy, outraged by the teasing. Simon hoped he hadn't sewn up that hole, that his precious soil was falling out all over this alien dirt.

Simon

Simon followed eagerly, herding them with his wishes. The quiet, long a habit, took no effort, and soon he became daring. Since Christopher had eyes only for his bear, sometimes Simon crossed moonlight, briefly startling against the night. He wanted to keep up.

Zoë dodged around the gazebo, up the steps on one side, and down those on the other side. There were four sets of steps; she used all but the one on the pit side. And Christopher chased her frantically, picking up speed, gradually casting aside the pretense. Soon he would be too enraged to care. He flung aside the knapsack that hindered his pace. It was a dark park, a late night—he'd strike quick and abandon the game.

Zoë was panting, and her face was white, as if the frost were tearing her throat. Dodge here. Duck there. Slowing down. And Christopher, on short, pudgy legs, moved faster, bouncing from step to step, across hollow boards, no fatigue on his face, only anger and growing bloodlust.

"Can't catch me," Zoë shouted between ragged breaths, and headed across the gazebo again to the other side. The side she had not gone down yet. The side with the pit.

Simon raced around the bushes, almost on all fours, and flung himself down in the dried leaves. He could see from here.

Zoë hit the top of the steps with a burst of speed. Suddenly she was in the air.

Oh, Zoë, don't jump too short. A picture of her, broken

and pierced, flashed through his mind. His hands went to his mouth to cover his horror.

Christopher was at the top of the steps, Zoë was flying through the air, and Simon felt frozen in time. He half rose.

Christopher, ready to run down the steps and snatch her, stopped. He had seen movement. His eyes focused in and found Simon, poised half free from the ground. Zoë rolled to safety as Simon and Christopher stared at each other, Simon in shock, Christopher in disdain.

Simon rose slowly, completing the journey to his feet. Zoë lay gasping on the grass, clutching the teddy bear to her like a talisman.

"What is your trick, Simon?" came the bell-clear child's voice, harder than any child's. "Have you a game afoot? Is this your slut?" He laughed when he saw Simon's eyes flash to anger. "Yes, how foolish I've been. I must be getting old. Where were you leading me, Simon?"

Simon relaxed a little, inwardly, but he wouldn't let Christopher see this. "That's for you to find out." Christopher didn't guess about the pit just a few short paces from him. There was hope.

"Shall I ask the girl?" Christopher's fangs glinted as he leered.

Simon wanted to hurt that face, slash it, rip it. His brother brought an unreasoning hate alive in him. It boiled inside him and made it hard for him to think. Caught in his anger, he didn't see the change right away.

Simon

"You cease to be amusing," his brother said. Christopher's voice was higher, wavering, as if his larynx was distorting. "I should have killed you long ago." It turned to a squeak.

Bullet fast, a black bat dived for Simon's face, over the pit, over the stake-lined hole that was to be its death. Sharp claws slashed at Simon's eyes, and he staggered out from the bushes, covering his face. He was only feet from the pit. The bat dived for his face again. Simon ducked. But the bat changed to a boy and sent Simon crashing to the ground.

They struggled furiously. Simon tried frantically to roll away from the pit that could be his own death, too, and Christopher unknowingly forced Simon closer.

Christopher was strong beyond human terms, yet so was Simon, and Simon was larger, which gave him more leverage. Yet Christopher lacked the spark of humanity that tempered Simon. He bit, he scratched, he clawed for Simon's throat, and won a throttling grip.

"You can't kill me," Simon gasped. "You have nothing you can kill me with."

"I can maim you," Christopher growled. "I can disable you and leave you helpless while I find the means." He sank his teeth into Simon's forearm and ripped the leather like tissue. He sliced the flesh beneath.

Simon screamed, more in anger than pain. "Damn you!" He clutched his brother's throat, but Christopher pried him off. Christopher rolled, and flipped Simon over him. Simon's head was over the edge of the pit.

A branch bent. Leaves rustled. Simon could hear the dirt trickle beside his ear as Christopher's weight bore down on him. Don't give, he begged the soulless dead boughs. He'll know then. He'll tip me over.

"Simon!" Zoë screamed. He had forgotten about her. She stood above them, beating at Christopher with a branch.

Christopher laughed in his blighted child's voice, the voice Simon hated so much. The branch broke. Tears ran down Zoë's face. Christopher began choking Simon again, crushing his windpipe.

Then another voice. "We've got you now, Blondie."

Christopher flung himself off Simon. "What the hell ...?" He crouched, ready to fight or flee.

Simon turned, and was amazed to see two boys running from the other side of the park—a big one, vaguely familiar, and a slighter, younger kid behind him.

They panted to a halt in front of Simon. Christopher backed carefully away. "Hassling kids now, pervert?" said the smaller boy.

Simon saw Christopher change his mind about running, a glint of interest in his eyes.

The bigger of the two advanced. "Kenny wants his jacket back, asshole."

The other followed. "Yeah. He'd get it himself, but he's still in the hospital."

Simon, furious at his plot's collapse, frustrated in his

anger, advanced on the boys, eyes blazing. Christopher could get away anytime he wanted now. Where would he go? How many more years would it take to find him again?

The big one pulled a knife from his belt—a cheap hunting knife honed to a brittle edge.

Simon stopped. He recognized the boy now. The fool. What made him think that he could do any better this time? But the smell of liquor drifting to him answered that question. Hunted him down, had they? Hunted the hunter?

The boy thought Simon had stopped from fear. He advanced, waving his knife, and Simon let him, anger raging inside. The lumbering boy was right before him now, but Simon stood his ground. The boy didn't know what to do. He had anticipated anything other than this. He swung his knife, expecting Simon to duck, but the blade slit neatly across Simon's face. Simon grinned a berserk grin. His fangs slid down from their sheaths. He licked his own blood.

The boy stepped back, his mouth open. He looked at the knife, and at Simon's face again, as if he couldn't believe what he saw. Then his eyes grew wide, and his tongue bulged like an idiot's. Simon felt his flesh pulling back together and knew what the boy saw before the boy turned and ran.

Simon whirled to face the other boy, who had crept around him during the confrontation, hoping to surprise him from behind. The boy gasped in horror as he saw the curtain of blood down Simon's face, the demonic leer, and the writhing flesh curling back into itself. He backed away, and a noise came from him like that from a wounded beast. Farther back he went. One step more. Then his arms were flailing, and he was sliding. There was a crash and a scream. He disappeared down into the pit, the hole meant for Christopher.

"You thought you could fool me with that?" Christopher smirked.

Simon moved toward him. I almost did, you bastard, he thought.

Zoë fumbled with her coat, as if burning up.

"I'll get away," hissed Christopher. "But I'll have your girl first."

He dived at Zoë, fangs bared. But something was in her hand—a crucifix. He stopped and snarled, raising his hands, then he started to shift. Leather wings peeled from his arms.

"Don't let him go," Simon screamed.

She blinked, too afraid to comprehend what he meant.

"Stop him!"

Christopher's face heaved and rippled. His nose turned up, and he began a mocking chitter.

Simon couldn't look at Zoë directly. The light coming from her upraised hand hurt his eyes. Yet he ran to her and grabbed the searing cross from her with a cry of pain. He hurled it at the creature that was Christopher, as it rose into the air. The ribbon tangled around the bat. The chittering turned to screams.

The boy emerged from bat, with the ribbon about his head, the cross strapped to his eyes. There were burns across his face, and he tore at his flesh as if trying to tear out the pain. He opened gouging wounds on his cheeks as he struggled over the grass. He couldn't see where he went. He stumbled blind. He stumbled too far, and he found the pit. He howled. A squelching thud filled the empty air where he had stood a moment before.

Simon flung himself down at the edge of the hole to see. He heard Zoë come up behind him, then moan and move back.

Christopher writhed on two stakes impaling him. Foul smoke arose from his bubbling form. His body, dying, tried remembered shapes to escape but couldn't quite make the change. A sequence of muddled forms emerged, and twisted on the skewers, spitting blood—boy with bat's head, wolf with boy's arms, pig with boy's face, sloughing skin.

And huddled in the corner, miraculously unhurt, the skinny boy whimpered and sucked his hands, too terrified to scream. Simon reached in, hauled him out with one hand, and flung him. He rolled across the grass, got up, and fled.

Christopher, a boy once more, twisted into a wizened dwarf, fell in on himself like a crushed insect husk, and finally lay still and mummylike.

Simon

Zoë didn't speak. Simon didn't turn to face her. He imagined disgust on her face and didn't want to see it.

"Leave me," he whispered hoarsely, fighting ice tears. "Leave me, brave heart. I'll come for you. I'll let you know how I am. I must fill this hole, and I must think."

He never turned to her. He never heard her leave. Or noticed the soiled teddy bear lying abandoned on the ground. The emptiness crashed in, and he asked himself the question that he hadn't dared to ask before. What will I do now?

· 15 ·

Zoë

Zoë gazed at her reflection in her mother's dresser mirror and held a string of pearls to her throat. They glowed against the black sweatshirt she was wearing. Her sleek neck showed no blemish, as if the boy had never existed, but he was out there somewhere. Her fingers trembled as again she felt the bitter aftertaste of sickness.

She'd come home last night and had hardly time enough to undress before she was in the bathroom throwing up. She'd huddled on the bathroom floor in her nightdress, pressing her sweating forehead against the cool porcelain, moaning with each wave of nausea. The repeated flushing finally got her father's attention, and he came tapping gently on the bathroom door. She let him in, and he patted her back and said comforting things, until she was well enough to get up and return to her room.

"Something I ate," she told him.

He laughed sympathetically. "You eat so little, it seems unfair."

She tried to smile. "Yes. It's usually me disagreeing with food, not the other way around."

Her sleep had been restless. Once she woke with a start in a cold sweat, but she couldn't remember what she'd been dreaming. She was afraid to fall back to sleep, fought it, in fact, but was dragged under again despite her efforts. She got up in the morning to a nervous stomach, and dark rings under her eyes.

"Don't go to school today, sweetheart," her father said before he went to work. "I'll pick you up here on my way to the hospital."

Zoë had no intention of going to school, but she couldn't settle to anything else either. Eventually, she found her way into her parents' bedroom, and to her mother's jewelry box.

She had always loved playing with her mother's jewelry when she was small, and her mother had sometimes used that to her advantage when she especially wanted some quiet. Going through the little drawers brought back the peace of childhood. Here was the cheap, sparkling star she had given her mother one Christmas, and here was her grandmother's ring. There was order in the rows of earrings under the velvet-lined lid, memories in the broken and odd assortments in their special niches.

But the old memories couldn't blot out her memory of the night before, and that awful, terrifying chase. She had

Zoë

really believed Christopher was killing Simon, and there was nothing she could do about it. I wanted to protect him, she thought. But how do you protect someone against that? The craziness was overwhelming her. And who were those boys? She shivered. Those stupid boys. She threaded the pearls back into their velvet pouch. They clicked like teeth.

Nothing will frighten me ever again after seeing Christopher in that hole, she decided. Her stomach tightened, still not immune to the memory. She closed the lid of the box.

Simon had killed his own brother. Surely that hurt, no matter what his brother had been? What did he feel? His whole life—if that's what you could call it—had been spent chasing this one thing. What would he do now?

If he leaves, could I go with him? she wondered. Could I live like that? She could live by night, she knew, but the blood? No, she couldn't face the blood.

Her gaze sought the self-portrait of her mother that hung over the bed. "He's so lonely," she said to the painting, as if begging her mother to understand.

She curled up on her parents' bed, stroking the familiar, nubbled bedspread, and fell asleep under the portrait, under her mother's watchful eyes. She slept an exhausted, dreamless sleep.

Her father found her still sleeping when he came home. She splashed some water on her face and climbed into the car, still bleary-eyed. They were almost at the hospital before she felt fully awake.

Zoë

Anne Sutcliff was sitting up in bed, wearing a pretty bed jacket she had bought on a trip to England years ago. She was very pale and thin, but she was smiling.

"I'm going to get a soda," Harry said. He left the room.

Zoë sat in a chrome chair by the bedside. She felt fragile.

"I hear you've been smashing up furniture."

Zoë started, and groped quickly for the excuse she had given her father. "Uh, yes. I put my coffee down without a coaster. You always warned me, didn't you?"

Zoë was relieved to see a familiar amused look on her mother's face. "Don't worry, no one's going to jump on you, silly. But I'm not sure a hot cup would have done quite that much damage."

"Well, it certainly was a surprise." Zoë felt herself redden.

"Zoë, I don't care what happened, really. You've a right to be angry."

God, she thinks I did it on purpose, Zoë thought.

"I used to get so mad," her mother said. "Not so much now."

Zoë remembered how, when her mother first got sick, she'd blow up at the tiniest thing. " 'Cause you were scared," she said.

"Yeah. That's part of it." Zoë's mother smiled at her. "But you can't keep it to yourself, or you burst at the seams. That's why I suggested the, you know, the therapist to your dad. When you said he wasn't talking."

"He went," Zoë said.

"You, too, huh? You're going to need each other."

When I'm gone, Zoë thought miserably, finishing the sentence for her.

Her mother reached for her hand and squeezed it, and her voice softened. "The world won't shatter, Zoë." She always seemed to know exactly how Zoë felt.

"We've all got to die," her mother whispered, and closed her eyes, as if admitting this had been a great effort.

Zoë cringed as if she'd been slapped. Don't talk about it, she pleaded silently. I don't want to talk about it. No matter how many times she'd told herself her mother was dying, it was awful to hear her mother say it. She stared at her jeans, afraid to look up.

Mom tugged at her hand. "It's not going to go away if you ignore it. There are no spells against death, Zoë."

Zoë forced herself to look at her mother. Yes, there are, she wanted to say. Dark spells. I know one. But she knew she couldn't. "You're giving in. If you say things like that, you're letting it happen."

Her mother shook her head. "I'm just not so afraid anymore. That's not giving in. Zoë, your dad's going to need help. You've got to look after him."

Zoë glanced at the door before she could help it. What if he heard?

Her mother saw the worry on her face and sighed. "I'm

189

sorry to put this on you. It's unfair, isn't it? You shouldn't have to be the strong one.''

Zoë's fists clenched. She was right, it was unfair. The whole thing was unfair. She finally asked the question she had kept on asking herself ever since this began. "Why you, Mom?"

Her mother took a clumsy sip of water. "It happens to people all the time, why not me? I'm not special. Hush!" She touched her lips. The gesture was an effort. "I know. To you. But not in the whole scheme of things."

Zoë looked at her mother with pride. She's so much better than me, she thought. She's brave.

"I don't think I could feel that way," she finally said.

"Well, people your age don't believe they can ever die."

Mom was quiet for a while. Zoë didn't know if she was resting or thinking. An orderly pushed a rattling cart by the door. Someone down the corridor was buzzing the nurse.

"I suppose I'm still a little angry," her mother finally said. "There's things I'd still like to do. Did I ever tell you how I wanted a house in the country with a bunch of cats, and a studio with huge skylights?"

"Lots of times." Zoë remembered sitting with her in the kitchen after school, when she took a break from painting. While they sipped hot tea, her mother would describe her perfect studio in minute detail. She never grew tired of planning it. Her mother could never live

Zoë

Simon's life—all nights, no bright, glowing days, no grand plans, only survival. She would pine, shrivel, become other than what she was. "What a half-assed life," she could imagine her mother saying, and she smiled.

Her mother looked at her curiously. "Something funny?"

"Cosmic humor."

"Oh." She didn't push. "Speaking of cosmic, I rather like the idea of reincarnation. I'd like to come back as a cat owned by someone like me."

Zoë took a deep breath. Maybe it got easier the more you talked about it. She'd try hard, for her mother's sake. "The someone like you would probably be married to someone like Dad, who's allergic."

Her mother's smile faded. "I can't comprehend being nothing. It gives me a spooky feeling inside."

That's what Simon said, Zoë realized.

Anne Sutcliff winced, squeezing her eyes shut, and Zoë's stomach did a flip. She wasn't going to die now? Right in front of her? But her mother composed herself.

"I can't go on with this pain."

Again Zoë thought of Simon.

"I was afraid that seeing me like this would wipe out the good memories, Zoë. That you'd only remember me like this. Don't let that happen. Remember when . . ." And she launched into one of her favorite stories of Zoë's childhood.

Zoë sat and nodded and smiled, and didn't really listen.

Zoë

She thought about what her mother had said. If she can deal with this, I'll try. But I don't have to like it.

Her father came back in and joined in with a story of his own. Then she was telling them her side of a story, and they were laughing, and she was a part of them again.

"Don't let it take away your life too," Zoë's mother whispered to her just before Zoë and her father left. "Live it for all it's worth while you've got it."

No, her mother could never live by night, in the dark.

"I'm glad you came," Dad said in the car.

There was still that thread between them. I just have to be patient, she realized. Let him grieve in his own way. Eventually he'll come back to me.

She let herself be mesmerized by the frosty circles around the streetlights. She felt full of happy and sad at the same time. Dad still needs me, she thought. And what about Lorraine? Just because she's out there doesn't mean she doesn't care anymore. It doesn't put her out of my life for good. She'll come back to me, too, in a way. No matter who she meets out there, we are still too much a part of each other's lives. I hope she calls me soon.

Things changed, she realized. People grew, they moved, they died. Sometimes they withdrew into themselves, and sometimes they reached out after needing no one. She remembered Simon's clinging embrace. What would it be like if nothing changed? she wondered. It would be stagnant, she supposed: frozen, decadent, terrifying. But why

Zoë

did it have to be so painful—all this change? Why did it mean losing people you love?

Then they were home.

There was a note on her bed, scribbled on a piece of paper torn from her notebook. *Meet me in the park at 12.* It was signed with a scrolling *S*.

She folded and refolded the note as she thought about him. He'd cheated death, yes, but was forced to live a life he hated. He was always shut out, never allowed to love, and was trapped in the horror of enslavement to his need for blood. She shuddered, thinking of the people he must have killed, and felt a little sick, knowing she had allowed him to kiss her.

But she felt different when he was there, when she could see the loneliness on his face. No matter what he'd done, he seemed innocent of it, like a wild animal. Now that he'd had his revenge, there was nothing left but the pain. He was too good to not be hurt by what he had to do to survive. He could never find happiness. A companion wouldn't make it easier. Death would be better than living that way. Sometimes there was a time for death.

She thought about her mother then. Perhaps there was always a good reason even if you couldn't see it, and it was a crime against nature to deny change.

Maybe it would be the kindest thing to kill him, she thought. No one else knew about him. Maybe it was her responsibility, for his sake, and the sake of others too.

She felt terrified at the very thought. But if she was

193

prepared to help kill Christopher, if she had been capable once, couldn't she be again?

In the garden shed she found a tumble of wood in the corner. Three thick shafts had been sharpened for some use in the yard. Their ends were darkened with soil. She held one and turned it in her hands. It would do. Her lip trembled, and her stomach twisted. Would she come from the front and see the look of betrayal on his face, or did she strike like a coward from behind? Did she even have the physical strength to force it through?

She flung the stake from her with a sharp cry, and its clatter echoed in the earthy hut. Simon wasn't like Christopher. She couldn't do it.

Zoë went to meet Simon after her father had fallen asleep on the couch. What am I to do? she thought. She passed a coarse, broken wall near a bus stop. Some semiliterate street poet had sprayed a message there: *Life is an ilusion that last too little*.

He was on her bench. He sat with his head bowed, and his eyes closed, like a choirboy in church. His translucent beauty once more surprised her. She could never quite remember it exactly, so it always came as a breathless shock. Beside him on the bench was his painting, on the other side a battered brown suitcase.

His head came up, and his eyes snapped open to meet hers. "Good evening," he said quietly. "Come sit with me." He put his suitcase on the ground. She went to him,

194

and he took her hand and kissed it. "Remember your poem, Zoë? I'm going to shift into a sunbeam this time."

She was puzzled and suddenly afraid for him.

"Wait with me for sunrise, Zoë."

Her eyes widened as realization slowly grew. "No. Don't." Despite her previous resolution she was struck with an overpowering desire to stop him, to offer her companionship to save him from this. She couldn't bear to lose him too. She reached for his other hand and held both his hands tight. She didn't have to say it. She didn't have to offer. He knew.

"No, Zoë. You are sweet and kind, but it would never work. It's my decision, isn't it?"

She knew he was right.

"I have stayed too long. Death is the nature of things." He looked away from her. "I am unnatural."

It was as if his thoughts had paralleled hers all along and so validated them. She leaned to him and kissed him on his cheek. He moved slightly, and his lips caught hers in a fleeting, delicate touch.

"What have I done, Zoë? Why did I exist?"

"You stopped Christopher. You even stopped von Grab. It was all worthwhile."

He let out a quick, crisp laugh of pleasure. "You are so generous. You're the only one in the world who knows or cares that I exist, and I can only bring you sorrow."

She let go of his hands. "Lately it seemed sometimes

that you were the only one who knew I existed. Soon I won't have anyone.''

He looked surprised. ''But you have yourself. A good, kind, strong, brave self. It was you who gave me courage.''

He stood and put the suitcase back on the bench; then he opened it, revealing gray, dry earth. He grabbed a handful and threw it to the air. She inhaled sharply. It was his life scattering. ''Help me, Zoë. I can't turn back.''

She hesitated. Then she stood too. Sometimes when things won't change, you have to force them. She took a tentative scoop and dribbled it through her fingers, but every grain cried out to her.

''No. Throw it,'' he demanded.

She scooped a large fistful and threw it as far as she could, screwing up her eyes against the sight. He's burning his bridges, she thought. I should be happy, but I ache.

He was flinging the earth every which way. He started to laugh, as if unburdened by a diminishing load. He threw faster and faster. She tried to keep up. Furiously, the dirt scattered through the air, thudded on the gazebo, spatted on the path, trickled through the slats of the bench. I can't stand it, she thought.

Then there were just a few crumbs left. Simon picked up the suitcase and, with a final wild cry, hurled it as far as he could into the bushes. He sank exhausted to the bench. Zoë settled beside him and took his hand again.

''Please keep the painting for me, Zoë. I want you to have it.''

Zoë

She touched the gilt frame in answer, accepting his gift, a piece of him always.

They sat in silence for a long while. Occasionally a car roared in the distance, miles telescoped by night. A mask of chill lay across her cheeks.

"I'm afraid," he finally said.

She slid her arms around him and held him tight, giving him her strength and love. This is all my mother wants, she realized.

The night was cold, but it wasn't the cold that trembled him in her arms. Now and then they kissed, then he would pull away and sigh. Sometimes he would stroke her neck longingly, place one kiss there, then lay his head on her breast. Once she saw he had tears in his eyes.

Birds began to sing here and there. The sky lightened to a pearly gray. She remembered Christopher in the pit and shuddered. Could she stand to see that again? Yet she held him tight. She wouldn't let him down.

Then the sun was rising.

They parted. Simon looked as if he might spring from the bench and run. She reached for him, and he almost fled from her touch, but he turned back and took her hand again.

He held ruthlessly still.

They didn't dare look anywhere but at each other as the sun rose higher. He flinched. She held her breath.

Then suddenly he was smiling. His face was lit by day

for the first time in three hundred years, and also lit by joy. He did not burn.

She wanted to laugh but dared not break the spell.

Instead, he began to fade. She held tighter, elation turning to dismay. Her fingers slid through his as if they were mist.

But his look of delight didn't change. "I think I'm free," he whispered. "All I had to do was go willingly."

She could barely see him now. He was just a shimmer, like ghostly heat rising from a long and lonely road. Her tears wouldn't stop. They flowed long after there was nothing but the memory of a faint voice.

"I love you, Zoë."

It's up to me now, she thought. But somehow it wasn't scary anymore.

ALSO BY
ANNETTE CURTIS KLAUSE

Turn the page for an excerpt from

AVAILABLE FROM DELACORTE PRESS

Published by Delacorte Press
an imprint of Random House Children's Books
a division of Random House, Inc.
New York

The morning was tentatively warm, and the smell of early roses drifted over from a neighbor's yard. The day would be hot later; she was glad she'd decided to wear shorts. *Not much school left now,* Vivian thought as she walked down the tree-lined street. *What will I do in the summer?* Move, she hoped. Get out of this place.

"Hey, Viv."

A lean, muscular figure peeled out from behind a stone gatepost, and her eyes widened briefly. "Rafe," she said in casual greeting, and kept on walking. If she hadn't been daydreaming she would have sniffed him out.

Rafe fell in beside her. She noticed that he was now cultivating a goatee and mustache. He ran a hand through his thick, long brown hair and shifted his grip on a package wrapped in newspaper he carried under one arm. "Going to school?"

"Some of us do."

The Five were more likely to be found hanging

out by the diner around the corner from school, or down by the river.

"Yaaaaahhhhhh!"

"Whooooooooooooooooo!"

Two boys dropped from a roadside tree in a jingling of chains, hair flying. This time she did start slightly, and cursed herself. She should have known the others were near. The twins, Willem and Finn, looked pleased with themselves. Round-faced Willem slipped an arm around her waist and gave her a friendly squeeze. "Didn't scare you, did we?" he asked, obviously hoping he had.

"You are such a puppy," Vivian said, removing his arm. He'd been her favorite of the twins as they were growing up. He was sweeter and more predictable than his brother, but his affectionate gestures had lost a great deal of their innocence in the last year or so.

Finn, the gaunter twin, smiled sardonically.

She was expecting the others now, so it came as no surprise when Gregory, the twins' lanky, fair-haired cousin, stepped silently out from behind another tree and folded in with them, and Ulf hopped over a white picket fence to dance his jittery way backward up the sidewalk, laughing wildly, until Rafe cuffed him to the rear.

They wore their usual uniform of boots, black jeans, T-shirts, and assorted tattoos. Rafe had his sleeves rolled up to show off his biceps. *My bodyguards*, Vivian thought.

"Saw your mother go into Tooley's bar with Gabriel

last night," Finn said. "She was all over him." His lips sketched a spiteful thin leer, and his eyes narrowed expectantly.

Vivian bristled, but she wasn't going to say anything.

"Yeah, Astrid wasn't far behind," said Rafe. "And she looked pissed." He laughed.

"Hey, leave my mom out of it," Ulf piped up.

So that's who they were fighting over, Vivian thought. *Gabriel.* That was disgusting. He was only twenty-four. And full of himself, from what she could tell.

Rafe took the parcel he carried out from beneath his arm, and Vivian heard Ulf giggle. Rafe pulled at the knotted string to loosen it. His eyes were more red than brown when he glanced up at her, a wicked grin playing about his lips, and Vivian knew he was up to mischief.

"Vivian, I'd like to give you my heart," Rafe said, suddenly serious, then immediately grinning again. "But since that might be inconvenient, I've brought you someone else's."

The newspaper unrolled, and he slapped a brown slimy gob down on the sidewalk.

"Rafe!" She looked around wildly, hoping no neighbors were in sight. "What the hell are you up to?"

The Five were helpless with laughter.

Vivian grabbed the newspaper from Rafe's hand and scooped up the mess.

"Give you my heart . . . ," he gasped, and bent over laughing again.

Where could she put this? Where was the body?

She started to rewrap the disgusting trophy. Then, "Rafe, you jerk," she cried. "This is a sheep's heart."

More howls of laughter exploded from the Five.

She didn't know whether to be angry or relieved. "You were over at Uncle Rudy's store, weren't you?" Rudy was a meat cutter at Safeway. When no one answered her, she growled and flung the whole package in Rafe's face. That set the others off even worse. Ulf had tears in his eyes.

She turned and left them, but they followed at a distance anyway, and she heard their bursts of laughter all the way to school.

Mom thinks the Five have learned their lesson, Vivian thought. "Hah!" she said out loud.

When Axel had come home from jail, her father had passed judgment swiftly. The punishment for endangering the pack was death.

Vivian couldn't save Axel, but she pleaded with her father for the Five. They were just kids like her. They had only killed to prove the witness wrong and protect the secret of the pack. They wouldn't do it again. So Ivan Gandillon made them beg forgiveness of the Moon and run the Trial of the Fang down a narrow path lined with the pack in their fur, and all could take their bites. Some said that he let the Five off too lightly, although they licked their wounds for weeks. Maybe those people were right. Vivian hadn't quite trusted the Five ever since.

It wasn't until almost lunchtime that Vivian remembered that she wanted to track down Aiden Teague.

Yeah, why don't I have a look at this poet, she told herself. *See if I like him writing about things he shouldn't know
about.* That was better than sitting around being miserable. Where should she look? She decided to ask her
art teacher. He was one of the advisers to *The Trumpet.*

"Oh, yeah. He's a junior," Mr. Antony said, shaking
some brushes out over the art-room sink.

"How would I find him?" Vivian asked.

"Well, if you hang around for another half an hour
until second lunch, all you'll have to do is look out that
window. He hangs out with his friends in the quad-
rangle, under those arches over there." He pointed
with the brushes to a section of the covered walkway
that ran around the perimeter of the square courtyard.

"What does he look like?"

"Oh, I dunno. He's tall, bohemian."

Whatever that means, she thought.

Mr. Antony must have noticed her blank look. "You
know, a throwback to the sixties, jeans and beads, an
MTV hippie."

The way he said that made her suspect that he
thought he'd been the real thing at one time.

"Oh, I know," the teacher added. "He was wearing
this flowery shirt this morning—lots of yellow and
blue. It made me smile. Listen, I've got to grab a sand-
wich. Close the door when you leave."

"Sure."

Luckily she'd brought her lunch with her. She
relaxed on the warm windowsill and chewed on a
piece of steak while she waited. Groups of kids were

scattered across the quad, eating, talking, and sun-bathing. Some of the boys had their shirts off, their flesh golden and slick as if they'd swallowed the sun. They were sweet to look upon. Her eyes lingered on them tenderly as she bit into her meat.

At the next bell, the shift changed. Kids reluctantly scooped up T-shirts, soda cans, and books, and hurried to class, while others hardly distinguishable from them took their places.

I'll be late to French, Vivian thought. It didn't matter, the teacher loved her. She had a perfect accent. Vivian sat upright, and her hands kneaded her empty lunch bag. She kept her eye on the arches.

Two young men walked into view. One had dark, shoulder-length hair and wore a flowered shirt. That must be him. Another boy joined them, then a girl. They stood laughing under the canopy, the shadows hiding their faces.

So that's you, Poet Boy, Vivian thought, but she couldn't see him clearly. She wanted a closer look.

Why am I bothering? she asked herself as she went through the side door. *Because I'm a pirate of the night and I want to see who's trespassing in my territory,* she answered. But maybe he was one of her kind from some other pack. *Or maybe he just knows too much,* she thought. She laughed aloud at her melodramatic thoughts as she crossed the grass, and a spotty tenth-grader eyed her curiously. The sun was hot, so she peeled off her shirt to reveal the tank top underneath.

Shall I only have a look, or will I say something? she wondered. *"Ooooh I loved your poem."* Instantly she felt like playing wicked games. She put a sway in her walk. *Maybe I'll make* him *look.*

The boy to Aiden's left noticed her first. He was a burly blond with a good-natured face and eyes that glazed over slightly at her approach. Vivian couldn't resist, she winked, and his cheeks turned pink. It was so easy. The other kid, wearing some kind of funny lopsided haircut, kept on yakking away, but the girl looked over and wrinkled her nose. She was small, with close-cropped dark hair—the sort of girl that wore black stockings even on days like these. *I'll put a few more runs in those tights, honey, if you look at me like that again,* Vivian promised silently.

Then Aiden Teague turned around to see what had captured his friends' attention. The crystal stud in his left ear reflected the sun in a burst of rainbow, and his slow easy smile sent a shock through her.

She was staring, she knew, but his face was delicious. His eyes were amused and dreamy, as if observing life from the outside and finding it vaguely funny. He seemed languid, not intense like the Five—those jangly, nervy, twitching, squirming, fighting, snapping, sharp-edged creatures who demanded so much from her. She noticed his tall dancer's frame and his long-fingered hands, and the thought crossed her mind that she would enjoy him touching her.

"Do I know you?" he asked. He waited expectantly, a bemused look on his face.

Vivian said the first thing that came into her head. "Um. I liked your poem in *The Trumpet*." *I don't believe that stupid sentence came out of my mouth,* she thought.

"Hey, thanks," Aiden said. He still looked puzzled.

He's not a werewolf, she thought in dismay. *How can I react this way when he's not one of us?* His smell of sweet perspiration and soap was purely human. *Get a grip, girl,* Vivian told herself. She didn't like this off-balance feeling. She put a hand on her hip and dared his dark eyes to try and drown her now. "Your poem was facing a print of mine. I was glad I wasn't next to some trash."

The blond kid brayed with laughter.

"Shut up, Quince," Aiden said, but he grinned.

"That was like some forest scene, wasn't it?" the kid with the funny haircut said. "Spooky, man."

The dark-haired girl put a hand on Aiden's arm. "Bingo's waiting for us."

"Hold on, Kelly." Aiden gently disengaged his arm, and the girl frowned sulkily. "Cool picture," he said to Vivian. "It's like you read my mind."

"That's what I thought about your poem," Vivian answered. Her response to him was disturbing but she wanted to explore it. She took his hand and turned it up, then ran her nails down the length of his fingers. He didn't resist.

"What are you going to do, tell my fortune?" Aiden asked.

"Yes," she answered. She slid a felt pen from her purse. Then, while he watched mesmerized, she wrote her phone number in his palm. On a whim she outlined it with a five-pointed star.

"What's that?" Quince said. "You Jewish or something?"

"Nah," said Aiden softly. "That's a pentagram."

"So she's a witch," Kelly snapped.

No, my dear, Vivian thought. *You don't watch enough late-night movies. The person who sees a pentagram in his palm becomes a werewolf's victim.*

"Are you a witch?" Aiden asked, his eyes twinkling.

Her voice was husky. "Why don't you find out?" She folded his hand around the sign that made him hers. Inside, her heart was thumping crazily in response to her charade, but she refused to lose her nerve.

As she walked away she heard Kelly raise her voice, but she didn't bother listening. Was that his girlfriend then? He could do better. Much better.

All afternoon her thoughts returned to him like a song she couldn't get out of her head. After a while it became annoying. *What am I, a pervert?* she asked herself. He was human, for Moon's sake—half a person.

It's only a game, she told herself, *to see if I can snare him.* But she wanted to know what was in a human head to make him write that poem, and she wanted to know why he'd stolen the breath from her lips.

As she reached home the front door opened. Gabriel, the inspiration for her mother's latest fight, was leaving. He filled the door frame, blocking her way. His T-shirt clung to his wide chest.

"Hi, Viv," he said. "Lookin' good." His voice rumbled like lazy thunder.

The teasing in his blue eyes made her want to spit. "Save that for Esmé."

Gabriel rubbed his chin and grinned. She noticed the puckered white scar tissue on the back of his right hand. The tip of another scar showed at his throat. "We don't see you down at Tooley's," he said, ignoring her anger.

She glared up at him. "I'm too young to drink."

He looked her over, taking his time. Before she could help it she tugged at the hemline of her shorts. Her shirt felt too tight. She was aware of a droplet of sweat that tickled its way down between her breasts. "Could have fooled me," he finally said.

She stared him in the eye, challenging him; she was out of her depth, but defiant anyway, willing her lip not to tremble. There was silence for a moment and she couldn't read his strong, chiseled face. He reached for her. She jerked back. Then he laughed like a giant and moved aside. She slid past him into the house, angry that she'd flinched, but showing him that she dared go by. She closed the door on his arrogant face.

"Mom!" she yelled shrilly.

Esmé poked her head out from the dining room.

"How long's he been here?" Vivian demanded.

"Only a few minutes," Esmé answered. She looked smug. "He dropped by to invite me for a late-night drink."

"Dammit, Mom. He's twenty-four."

"So?"

"You're almost forty."

"Well, rub it in." But nothing was wiping the smile off Esmé's face.

"Don't you think it's a little bit disgusting?"

Esmé flung her hands in the air. "Well, for goodness' sake, I'm not serious about him."

"Oh great. Now he's your boy toy."

Esmé smirked. "Some boy." She danced up the stairs, her rear end wagging like a tail. Vivian followed Esmé up and slammed the door of her room.

Rudy had gone to Tooley's bar after work, so there were just Vivian and Esmé at the dinner table. Vivian was still brooding about Gabriel's visit. She thought of her father and the aching emptiness that still gnawed at her. Her parents had seemed so happy together. She'd thought her mother shared that ache, but now Esmé was acting like a stupid fourteen-year-old.

"Didn't you love Dad?" she finally said.

Esmé looked startled at this question out of the blue. "Yes, I loved him."

"Then why are you out running around?"

"A year's a long time, Vivian. I'm tired of crying. I'm lonely. Sometimes I want a man in my bed."

Vivian grabbed her plate abruptly and headed for the kitchen. Couldn't her mother talk to her as if she was a daughter? She scraped her leftovers into the trash with a squeal of knife against porcelain.

"Watch those dishes!" her mother yelled.

That's more like it, Vivian thought.

An hour later Vivian was on her bed doing some halfhearted studying for Chemistry, when the phone rang. She picked up the phone on the second-floor hallway, expecting to hear one of the pack, but it was Aiden.

"There's a free concert at the university this weekend," he said. "Sunday afternoon. You wanna go . . . maybe?"

Her eyes half closed and she licked her lips. "Maybe. Who's playing?"

He mentioned a band she'd never heard of in reverent tones that suggested it was well known and one of his favorites. He was sharing a special treat with her. "I'll have to see if my family has anything planned," she told him. "I'll let you know tomorrow." No sense in letting him think her too eager. "No. Don't worry. I'll find you."

Vivian hung up and stretched her arms to the ceiling contentedly, arching her back. Should she go, or was having him rise to the bait good enough?

But a shadow slid across her pleasant mood. If they went on a date he would want to kiss her. Would he be safe if he came close enough to fill her nostrils with his scent?

Esmé walked out of her bedroom. She was wearing

the tight black dress she used for waitressing. "Who was that?" she asked casually as she put in an earring.

"A boy from school."

Esmé paused. "Oh?"

"He asked me to a concert."

"One of *them* asked you out?" Her mother's expression combined repulsion and surprise. "I won't allow it."

Vivian bristled. "You can't tell me who to date."

Esmé put her hands on her hips. " 'Don't date if you can't mate,' the saying goes." Human and wolf-kind were biologically incapable of breeding.

"I'm going to a concert, not having his baby," Vivian snapped. "And don't tell me wolf-kind only start relationships when they want children. I know better."

"You've got a smart mouth, girl," Esmé called as she walked off.

Now Vivian was sure she was going.

He had phoned, and she wasn't an outsider anymore—untouchable and strange, perhaps invisible. But why should she care so much? He *was* a human after all: a meat-boy scantily furred, an incomplete creature who had only one form.

How sad, she thought, and suddenly she craved the change.

Like all her people, at the full moon she had to change whether she wanted to or not, the urge was too strong to refuse. Other times she could change at will, either partway or fully. Right now the moon swelled like a seven-month belly, and she wanted to change because it was possible. She wanted to run for the joy of it.

She stalked through the backyard dusk, across the bat-grazed clearing in the narrow ribbon of woods out back, over the stream, up the embankment, and down into the wide grassy valley that held the river.

The grass was already high. Here and there might be nests made by kids making out or getting high, but she sniffed the air and smelled no human flesh.

Down by the river was a giant tumble of rocks that screened the riverbank. Behind the rocks, amid the shoulder-high weeds, she slowly slid off her clothes. Already her skin prickled with the sprouting pelt. A trickle of breeze curled around her buttocks, and her nipples tightened in the cool air off the river. She laughed and threw her panties down.

Her laugh turned to a moan at the first ripple in her bones. She tensed her thighs and abdomen to will the change on, and clutched the night air like a lover as her fingers lengthened and her nails sprouted. Her blood churned with heat like desire. *The night,* she thought, *the sweet night.* The exciting smells of rabbit, damp earth, and urine drenched the air.

The flesh of her arms bubbled and her legs buckled to a new shape. She doubled over as the muscles of her abdomen went into a brief spasm, then grimaced as her teeth sharpened and her jaw extended. She felt the momentary pain of the spine's crunch and then the sweet release.

She was a creature much larger and stronger than any natural wolf. Her toes and legs were too long, her ears too big, and her eyes held fire. *Wolf* was only a convenient term they had adopted. Those who preferred science to myth said they descended from something older — some early mammal that had absorbed protean matter brought to Earth by a meteorite.

Vivian stretched and pawed at the ground, she sniffed the glorious air. She felt as if her tail could sweep the stars from the sky.

I will howl for you, human boy, she thought. *I will hunt you in my girl skin but I'll celebrate as wolf.*

And she ran the length of the river to the edge of the city slums and back, under the hopeful early-summer moon.